# PUNDRAGON

## CHANDRA K. CLARKE

FRACTAL MOOSE PRESS

Copyright © 2020 Chandra K. Clarke.
www.ChandraKClarke.com

Dr. Seuss "Cat in the Hat" quotation used with permission.
Cover design by Tiger Maple Publishing & Go On Write
Book Design by Tiger Maple Publishing
Published by Fractal Moose Press, an imprint of Tiger Maple Publishing
www.TigerMaplePublishing.com

978-1-7772174-1-9 (paperback)
978-1-7772174-0-2 (ebook)

*Pour changer la façon commune de penser.*

– Diderot

*I*t was dark.

Pitch black, in fact.

And it *had* been quiet. Really, really quiet.

Until now.

There was a loud popping noise, followed by a long, low hissing sound. The air crackled as though electrified.

Somewhere in the distance, a low whistle pierced the air. As the seconds ticked by, it got louder and the pitch got higher. Louder and louder, higher and higher, like an incoming missile, and then—

*Whompf.*

It wasn't a loud *whompf* nor even a particularly impressive one. Actually, it was kind of soft and squishy. But the whistling stopped.

A second or two later, the *whompf* was followed by a loud crash. The kind that you might hear if you had dropped a garbage can lid in the dead of the night and it landed at just the right angle to allow it to roll around and around and around until it finally clattered to a noisy stop.

There was another pop and another hiss. A dog barked uncertainly. Then, there was silence.

In the darkness some minutes later, something sighed.

"Oh, *bother.*"

# PART I

*I*an glared at the underside of his kitchen sink.

It was broken, like practically everything else in the house, and the coupling nuts securing the trap and the tailpiece were corroded and refusing to budge. But the drain was extremely clogged, and no amount of plunging, chemical attacks, or poking about with the drain auger had done the trick. There was nothing for it, but to take it to pieces.

Ian squared his shoulders, set the wrench up, tightened it, and heaved. The nut held for a good five seconds. Ian's forearm bunched and strained, and his face started to redden.

The nut disintegrated.

With nothing to hold on to, the wrench swung sideways, smashing into the shutoff valve handle with a loud clang. Ian struggled out from underneath the sink, cursing and rubbing his hand. That was probably going to leave him with a fine bruise later, but at least the hard part was over. He wondered if he still had an ice pack in the freezer.

Everything below the sink vibrated ominously, and the valve made a loud *thunking* noise. Water suddenly surged back into the faucets, blowing the spout straight up into the air on a plume of hot water. Mouth agape, Ian watched as it banked off the ceiling at an angle and came crashing down on the side of the kitchen radiator, breaking off the air release vent there. The radiator began fizzing and spitting brackish, smelly, rust-coloured water all over the floor.

Not to be outdone, the sink, already mostly full from the morning's dishes, overflowed, spilling soap and grey muck. A splash of hot water from the fountaining faucet splatted Ian right above the eyebrow.

"Ow, ow, *ow!*" he yelped, scalded into action. He dived under the sink again and banged on the shutoff valve with his fist until the water finally turned off. The resulting water hammer made the whole plumbing system shudder. The radiator hissed and spat a few more times before subsiding, having emptied itself. The flow of water from the sink onto the floor dwindled into a fitful trickle.

Ian looked at the dent in his ceiling with a mixture of awe and bemusement. He had thought that sort of thing only happened in the movies or TV comedy skits.

He squelched away from the mess and sat at his tiny Formica-clad table, staring out the window in a daze. Across the street, his neighbour, Mrs. Mabel Ann Wilson, was already out and weeding her amazing flower garden in the early morning sun. The word "Monday" floated across his consciousness. It was followed by the words "work" and "council meeting, 7 a.m." His eyes flicked to the clock on the wall; it read 6:30. He groaned and put his head in his hands.

As the lone reporter for *The Express*, it was Ian's job to cover the news and special events in Teisburg, Ontario—population 4,200. Of all the assignments he had to do, he hated council coverage the most. The meetings were very long, extremely boring, and generally didn't get much accomplished. He eyed the sodden mess that was his kitchen and considered calling in sick.

On cue, his phone vibrated into alertness on the table.

"Hello?"

"Don't even *think* of calling in sick today, Ian."

It was Janice Halton—publisher, owner, and editor of *The Express.*

He decided to give it his best shot. "But I feel horrible," he said. "I can't even haul myself out of bed!"

"Nonsense," Janice replied. "You're in your kitchen and have been for at least half an hour."

Ian sighed, stood up, and moved closer to his kitchen window, phone in hand. Immediately, Mrs. Wilson spotted him and waved as cheerily as only morning people can at that hour. He wondered if she'd even had any coffee yet.

"What? She has a direct hotline now? A psychic connection? I didn't even see her go into the house."

"Well, if you must know," Janice said, "I just got off the phone with her a few minutes ago. I wanted to get details on the flower show this Wednesday. And her son just bought her a cell phone on the weekend. Didn't she tell you?"

"Great. Whose bright idea was it to give the town's biggest gossip a cell phone?"

"Don't be snide, Ian. She's a great source for the paper. Her son wanted her to have a mobile phone, as she's getting up there in age, you know."

Ian snorted at this and rubbed a hand across his face, smearing grungy water and muck from the pipes across it in the process. "She's in better physical shape than half the town. No worries there. And I have to be snide since you're not buying the sick story."

"Wouldn't matter if you were at death's door. You can't miss this morning's meeting. The recycling motion is coming up under 'new business.' We're slack for the front page, and this will be a good story."

"Be still my heart," he muttered.

"I heard that. Listen, it's not anti-government protests or terrorist bombings, and thank goodness for that, but it is important, okay? Just be there. Oh, and don't forget the meeting is at the dealership this week. It's the third Monday of the month and—"

"—And Larry takes in his new inventory right after the meeting. I know. You've told me this."

"Sorry, it's just that I can never tell how much of this kind of thing you take on board. You've been here two years, and yet you never seem to know any personal details or relationships or anything around here."

"I have this fond hope that if I keep out of everyone else's business, they'll keep out of mine."

"Ian you grew *up* in a small town. You know that we'll keep gossiping and you'll miss out on the good stuff. Now go hit the shower, or you'll be late." *Click*.

He surveyed the wreckage in his dripping kitchen. "Already had one."

\* \* \*

Ian Laughlin MacDonald looked like his name. That is to say, he was almost stereotypically Scottish: red hair, green eyes, and fair skin with just a dusting of freckles. He had his father's strong build but not his strong brogue: northern Canada had already called to the MacDonalds by the time Ian was born.

Which is why Ian hated mornings. It was hard to be enthusiastic about the day when it was -30C outside and pitch black for a good chunk of the year. Well, okay, it was hard to be enthusiastic about pretty much *anything* under those conditions, but mornings were especially bad in the north, and his loathing of them had followed him south.

It was also why Ian didn't like small towns much. His father had worked first in oil, then in logging, and finally in teaching, moving farther and farther north to smaller and smaller towns. By the time Ian had finished high school (online, of course), they were living north of the sixtieth parallel in Fort Simpson, Northwest Territories.

So, when the University of Toronto had accepted his application for an English undergrad degree, Ian couldn't move south fast enough. Warmth! Crowds! Coffee on every corner! Yet, after a little more than six years, fate had conspired to set him down in yet another tiny municipality.

* * *

Ian hurriedly pulled on some clean, dry jeans, a grey shirt, and his battered black canvas running shoes. He burned the toast, knocked over the large pile of unpaid bills on the table, threw every towel he had down on to the floor of his half-flooded kitchen, and opened some windows to let in a drying (he hoped) breeze. He threw himself into his ancient pickup truck, cursed it into starting, and roared down the road, trying to ignore the smelly, dark exhaust coming out of his tailpipe.

The meeting, as Janice had reminded him, was at Larry's car dealership. While Larry lived in town, his business was actually a few kilometres into the country. Paving quickly gave way to kidney-bruising washboard gravel lanes.

Larry—not to be confused with his cousin Harry, who was the town's first black mayor, or his twin brother, Frank, the farmer. They were probably all related in some way to Mrs. Wilson, although Ian hadn't figured out how yet. Mrs. Wilson seemed to be related to everybody.

Even though it was spring, it was already quite warm. Ian wiped a hand across his upper lip. He wasn't looking forward to another summer of Ontario's heat and wicked humidity. They were hard on a northerner, even after all the time he'd been down here, and it seemed like they'd been getting worse.

As little towns went, Ian supposed, Teisburg was a good place. It had wide, tree-lined streets, pleasant, well-tended homes, and friendly people. It had a large plot of land set aside for a nature preserve and another for a recreational park. Teisburg kids played soccer there every summer. The hockey arena doubled as a community centre whenever the ice was off, and there was a community pool that had recently been converted to salt water. The bustling downtown (or uptown, as they called it here) included a tavern, a Chinese restaurant, a fried-chicken franchise, a ridiculous number of gas stations given the size of the place, a flower shop, and a hardware store. The stately old town hall had elevator access to the council chambers but a dysfunctional bell in the clock tower. All parents sent their children to the public school in town, the tiny Catholic school having finally been shuttered the previous year after decades of dwindling attendance. Older kids were bused into the nearby city to attend high school.

And the countryside surrounding Teisburg was always pretty at this time of year, with everything greening up. Farmers were experimenting with regenerative agricultural techniques, combining livestock and crop farming, setting aside their plows in favour of no-till cover crops and residue grazing. Even old Frank was playing around with strips of wildflowers in his fields, bringing in natural predator insects to cut his pesticide costs. Ian rolled his eyes every time Frank held court at the coffee shop, bragging about last season's yields as he tucked into yet another doughnut. Few are more evangelical than the recently converted.

Ian's pickup bumped and rattled down the road, crunching through the gravel. He checked his watch and relaxed a bit, thinking he'd make it to the meeting with a few minutes to spare.

And then his tire blew.

The blowout was so loud and so sudden that the truck swerved sideways and began skidding toward the ditch. Ian grappled with the steering wheel and slammed on the brakes.

The truck swung around violently, rocking high up on two wheels for one terrifying moment before bouncing back down.

When he could breathe normally again, he pried his fingers from the steering wheel and got out to inspect the damage. The right front tire was in ribbons. Bits of shredded rubber lay all over the road. The rim itself was dented, but it looked like it could still take a tire.

He traced the rubber bits back up the road, picking them up as he went, until he found what looked like a metal plate. It was about a metre wide and nearly teardrop-shaped. The plate was an iridescent pinkish-red colour, quite thick, and had a tip that was bent up to a nasty point. A small piece of black tire rubber clung to the sharpest edge.

Ian briefly wondered if Monday was trying to kill him.

He glanced at his watch and swore yet again, gathered up the debris, including the plate, and heaved it all into the back of the truck. Then he began hunting in the cab for a jack and tire iron.

* * *

The council meeting didn't end until 11:30 a.m., so by the time Ian rolled into *The Express* parking lot, he was tired, bored, and hungry. A former gas station converted into an office, it was made of plain cinderblocks painted light blue and had a flat roof and two large windows looking out onto the street. Its two garage bay doors were permanently locked and painted a slightly darker shade of blue. It wasn't well insulated, so they tended to freeze in the winter and roast in the summer; right now, it was still fairly pleasant inside.

The main door chimed as he walked into the building.

Suddenly, he was enveloped in a cloud of brightly coloured paper confetti.

"SURPRISE!"

Ian stopped, blinking. Tiffany Dunlop, office administrator, bookkeeper, and general dogsbody for the paper, was standing behind the reception counter, beaming at him. Her hair was currently in a messy updo, and her blue eyes sparkled with mirth.

He groaned and closed his eyes briefly. It was official. Monday *was* trying to do him in.

He pasted on a smile and opened his eyes. "I can't believe you remembered that it was my birthday today."

Tiffany came around the counter and gave him a hug. "Couldn't miss this one, could we? The big three-oh, after all! How does it feel?"

"Uh, same as twenty-four does to you, I guess?"

"Lots more candles on your cake though."

"Cake? Did you say cake?"

"Yes, I did. But you can't eat any until after lunch. I brought sandwiches in for everyone today in your honour." She glanced out the front window. "Oooh, look! Here comes the courier guy! He's bringing in our new wedding invitation order book. I can't wait to see the new styles!"

Ian avoided the delivery and headed for Tiffany's desk. Sure enough, amid the pictures of unicorns, puppies, and family, there were sandwiches. He scooped a couple, grabbed the chair from his own desk, and wheeled it around to face the office.

The paper's ad salesman and comp artist, Melvin Jacobs, was on the phone. "Hi, Michael. It's just me," he said in a doleful voice. "You wouldn't be interested in the three-by-five this week, would you? No? Well, you won't want the three-by-four. Oh? All right. I'll put you down for that." There was a pause while he made a careful notation. "What's that you say? I don't know. Hold on there just a minute. Hey!" he said to the office without bothering to mute the phone. "Can we do cats?"

"I've got pictures of Tibbles and Nibbles," Tiffany said doubtfully.

There was a frustrated sigh from the main office—a small, walled-off corner of the building. Janice poked her head around the door.

"We pay an exorbitant amount of money for monthly access to a database of royalty-free stock photos and clip art. There will be sitting, standing, playing, and sleeping cats. Any size, any shape. And, Melvin, will you please, *please* put the phone on hold in situations like this? Can we at least try to be professional here?" She disappeared from the door.

Melvin went back to his conversation. "Yeah, we can do cats." Another pause. "That's fine. Talk to you on Friday at the card party." He set the phone down and motioned to Tiffany. "He likes Nibbles best."

"I *heard* that," Janice said.

Melvin chuckled and nodded at Ian. "Happy birthday. My Elinor says the same."

"Sandwich?" Ian offered between mouthfuls.

"I thank you," Melvin replied and stood to reach for one. He raised his voice a little. "Janice dear, come in and eat."

Janice reluctantly came out for lunch. "Tell me why I put up with you."

Melvin adjusted his black horn-rimmed glasses and smoothed back his short, grey hair. "You cannot live without my long years of experience and wisdom. And charm."

"Besides, he came with the paper," Ian said.

"Hmph," Janice said and sat down. She was dressed in pristine khaki pants and a dark purple summer blouse that set off the deep brown colour of her skin. She had recently taken to styling her hair into a short fade with the hair on top dyed a bright green. An urban girl who came from a life of suburbs and strip malls, she'd bought *The Express* three years ago with savings from her job as a city staff reporter. Born into the Internet era, she somehow seemed to have printer's ink for blood and had resisted going completely digital with the paper. "How are we doing for ads?"

"Just fine, young lady. Now come and eat a sandwich. Before I retire, I am going to teach you how to take breaks."

"Janice has what you call a 'type A' personality, Melvin," Ian said, pulling out a low desk drawer and propping a foot up on it. "Breaks aren't an option."

"Spare me the psychology," she said. "It has more to do with my lonely old bank account than anything classified according to the alphabet. Happy b-day, by the way. You're catching up."

"You still have a couple of years on me."

"And I bet you won't ever let me forget that."

Ian raised a sandwich half in a cheers motion. "I'll do my level best."

Tiffany scooted over in a chair, wedding invitation book in hand. "Wow. There's just tons of new stuff. Their new premiere line looks *so* cool."

"Poor James doesn't have a chance," Melvin said with a smile.

"Jamie called about you this morning," Tiffany said to Ian, brightening. "Said he missed you at the dealership but to tell you that he's got used tires at the back if you want one."

Jamie, who had been Tiffany's boyfriend since grade eleven, was Melvin's great-nephew and Larry's mechanic.

"How does he know I need a tire?"

"He saw you drive away with a doughnut on your wheel."

"Figures. I'd forgotten about it."

"How was the council?" Janice asked.

"Long. But there'll be about six stories from it."

"Good. I've got a four-inch hole on the front page."

Ian choked on the remainder of his sandwich. "Four inches? I thought you said we were slack?"

"That was this morning. And you needed the motivation. Anyway," she said, selecting a couple of sandwiches, "when you're done with writing all of that up, come back and help me, would you? I've got page seven ready to lay out this afternoon, and we have some job work on the platen press. Business cards for the hardware store, I think." She disappeared back into her office, nibbling her lunch as she walked.

Melvin leaned over conspiratorially. "I hear she's looking to buy another paper . . . maybe in Essex County."

"Who'd you get that from?" Tiffany asked.

"I hate doing work on the platen press," Ian said. It was an ancient Gordon type with an enormous flywheel. "It keeps trying to eat my fingers."

"The bank manager," Melvin replied.

"My cousin said it was likely one on the other side of London."

"Which cousin? Susan?"

"Why is she thinking of buying another paper? What happened to buying a heavy-duty laser printer so we can recycle the flat bed?" Ian said. "It's out to get me, I swear."

"No. Freda."

"Hmm, can't trust Freda to get her stories straight. She probably meant the other side of Leamington," Melvin said, pushing up his glasses.

"Is anyone listening to me?"

"The new printer's on back order, Ian. Have some cake, and quit complaining." Tiffany patted him on the shoulder. The phone rang. "Good *afternoon*! This is the *Teisburg Express*. How may I help *you* today?"

Ian looked at Melvin. "You know, sometimes I swear I can

hear the heart-shaped dots over the letters 'i' and 'j' when she talks."

\* \* \*

Ian worked until well past six in the evening, finishing up his stories, running the business cards, and setting up pages seven through twelve of the week's edition of *The Express*.

When he got back to the house, he found a copy of *Architectural Digest* tucked inside his front door. He sighed. When he'd first moved to Teisburg, real estate pickings within his budget had been slim. There had been a musty apartment over the variety store, a small clapboard rental home on Oak Street, and an old brick home that had supposedly once belonged to a retired saddlebag preacher, one of the founders of the town. At the time, it had seemed like a good idea to buy, rather than rent and have nothing to show for his money when he eventually escaped Teisburg. The real estate agent had told him it had "character."

That same agent and had probably dined out for a week on the story of having finally unloaded the local money pit to the "kid from Tronna."

Meanwhile, some kind soul kept dropping off restoration guides and inspirational magazines, thinking Ian was trying to restore the house to its former glory. Mostly, he was just trying to keep it from falling on his head.

He tossed the magazine onto the last bare spot on the kitchen table and spent the next hour properly cleaning up the morning's mess. When he finished that, he grabbed some cold pizza from the fridge, wandered into the living room, sat down in the room's only chair—a second-hand recliner—and pulled his aging laptop out from underneath it. He cranked the chair lever to pop the footrest, leaned back, and ate while waiting for the computer to boot up.

On the other side of the living room was a shelf devoted entirely to swag from his time at WizardSoft. There was a ball cap with the WizardSoft logo, a set of framed game decals, a replica stun gun made by a dedicated fan and cosplayer and sent to Ian personally, a deluxe edition of *Homicida* still shrink-wrapped in its box, and various pictures of Ian at the launch party for the game.

*His* game. A grimdark dieselpunk massively multiplayer masterpiece, according to *The Toronto Star*. A runaway best-seller, said *PC Gamer*. Concept and story by I. L. MacDonald.

Career set. Or so you'd think. One corporate merger and a redundancy slip later, he was out of a job. Nine months of unemployment and Toronto rent had chewed through his meagre savings like they were so much butter. Meanwhile, the new owners of *Homicida* continued to rake in monthly subscription fees.

And so here he was in Teisburg, because any job was better than no job and it was far cheaper to live here than it was even in the outskirts of the Greater Toronto Area. Plus, he still had his massive student loans to pay off. All he had to do now was write another game storyline. Only this time, he'd sell it or license it to a studio for royalties. No more work-for-hire contract clauses for him . . . no, sir.

The computer finished booting up. He opened the word-processing software, took another bite of his pizza, cracked his knuckles, put his hands on the keyboard, and . . . waited.

He tried staring at the ceiling for a while. It was the best ceiling in the house, as it was the only one without cracks or, more worryingly, water stains. He finished the pizza. He finished the crust. He attended to several crumbs. Little beads of sweat appeared on his forehead. But the screen remained resolutely blank, and the little blinky-flashy line on the page went blithely on with its business, blinking and flashing and mocking him. He felt like swearing at it and wondered if that was why it was called a cursor.

Ian stayed like this for two hours, slowly losing even the desire to fidget. He stopped when the power-saver feature finally made the screen go dark and he caught a glimpse of his reflection: he looked like a deer caught in the headlights. A thirty-year-old deer, apparently developing some serious under-eye baggage.

Drained and exhausted, he slouched back into the dark, still slightly damp kitchen to get a root beer. He leaned against the window frame in time to see Mrs. Wilson come flying into her driveway on her European-style bike, dismounting neatly while it was still moving. Returning from one of her many committee meetings, no doubt. Ian took a pull of his drink and hoped she couldn't see him.

\* \* \*

His phone rang, startling him out of his funk. Ian smiled when he saw the caller.

"Hey, Mom," he said.

"Hello, luv. It's not too late, is it?"

"No, no. I was just thinking about going to bed but hadn't yet."

"Ah, good. Happy birthday. Your dad said he might call you later in the week. He's at a conference in Whitehorse. Did you go out with your mates tonight?"

Ian's eyes grew moist, and suddenly his movements sounded loud in the empty house. He cleared his throat. "Uh, no. It, ah, it was a work night. They had sandwiches and cake for me at the office today, though."

"Ah, that's lovely. How are things otherwise? You sound a bit fashed."

"Oh, you know . . . it's been a long day. Mondays are usually pretty rushed as we go to print at noon tomorrow."

His mother made a clicking noise with her tongue. "Och, that sounds so old fashioned. It would be so much easier just to run it like a blog. They've been doing it that way up here for years."

Ian nodded. "Yeah, I know. Janice does too, but she says that there are enough older residents who still like the paper version that it's still financially viable. We'll start putting out a digital version later this year, I think. Not sure how she's going to make that pay."

"Hmm. And what else is bothering you? The longer I hear you talk, the more down you seem."

Ian sat at his table and fiddled with some of the papers there. "Nothing. Same old, same old." He blew out his cheeks in frustration. "I guess it's just that this is not where I thought I'd be by thirty."

"What's wrong wit' where you're at?"

"Everything!" Ian snapped. He could practically hear his mother's disapproval in the silence that followed. "Sorry. It's just that I've got a dead-end job, I'm stuck in a tiny town again, I'm in debt up to my eyeballs, this house has a repair list longer than my arm, my truck is a stinking polluting heap—"

"You still have that awful truck?"

"Yes," Ian replied. "And don't even get me started on how hard it is to sleep with all this political stuff going on and climate change and—"

"Aye, and what are you doin' about it all?"

"If I could just get another game idea—"

"So yer sittin' and waitin' for that muse again, eh?"

"No! I'm not . . . I'm not waiting. I've been trying to write. I'm just so tired when I get home."

"Oh wheesht," said his mother, shushing him. "Ye know, there are days when I rue ever having givin' ye comic books to read."

Ian could hear her accent thickening, as it usually did when she became frustrated with him. "What do comic books have to do with this?"

"Because ye seem to be waitin' around for a superhero to come and save ye."

"I'm not!"

"Y'are," she said firmly. "D'ye not remember a thing about how I taught ye to clean yer room?"

"What?" Ian pinched the bridge of his nose.

"You used to let your bedroom get into such a state. And I'd send you to go and sort it, and you'd stand there in the middle without a clue until I came and quoted Dr. Seuss at you."

Ian smiled at the memory in spite of his mood. He recited the lines to her:

*"And this mess is so big*
*And so deep and so tall,*
*We cannot pick it up.*
*There is no way at all!"*

"Right. You'd never know how to get started. And I'd tell you to focus on one thing that you *could* do in that room, like straighten out your bookshelf. And then to focus on another thing, and another, and so on, and before you'd know it, the room would be done."

"But I *am* focused on one thing! Once I have my next game idea . . ."

"And what if that idea doesn't come for another five years? Or doesn't come at all?"

"Gee . . . thanks, Mom. That's real inspiring."

"Hoping is not a plan, Ian. You can't just go banging around from pillar to post, head down, prayin' it'll all resolve itself. Sit ye down, figure out what you want, and go at it piece by piece until you make it happen. And if one piece isna workin', get on with somethin' else."

"Just like that, eh?"

"Just like that," his mother said. "It's the only way to get things done."

Ian was silent a moment and then said, "Yes, well . . . thanks for calling, Mom. I look forward to hearing from Dad later."

"I love you, Ian. You know that."

"I know, Mom. Talk to you soon."

He shut off his phone and stared morosely out into the darkness for a while. Then he locked up the house and fell into bed.

* * *

At around midnight, Ian opened his eyes. It was a full moon outside, and he'd forgotten to close the curtains. He rolled over to get out of bed and—

There was a dragon in his bedroom.

He closed his eyes.

Cold pizza, he thought, had a lot to answer for.

He lay there for a bit, more than a little weirded out. Perhaps he was dehydrated. A glass of water might help.

Still keeping his eyes closed, he sat up slowly, did a couple of stretches, and yawned.

Then he worked up the courage to open his eyes again. The dragon was still there.

"Hello," it said.

At a little after midnight, Ian passed out.

\* \* \*

Ian came to, looked around, and shut his eyes firmly. He was in the process of peeking for a third time when the dragon became annoyed.

"Oh, stop that," it said crossly. "Let's take it as a given that when you open your eyes, I will *still be here*. Can we move on from that?"

Ian cautiously sat up again. It wasn't that he agreed with the dragon necessarily, but he figured that sitting up might be better than being completely prone when next to a grumpy dragon.

"You," he said, glad that his voice sounded steady, "are a figment of my imagination."

The dragon sounded excited. "Really? The theory of transdimensional psychokinetic hysteresis is actually true?"

Ian looked blank.

"Riiight," the dragon said. "Let's start with the basics." It cleared its throat. "Me dragon, you not."

Still sleepy, Ian nodded. "Okay."

"I have a problem. You're going to help me."

More alert, Ian said, "Why would I do that?"

"More basics: me big, you little."

"Is that a threat?"

"No. It's a subtly worded construction designed to elicit optimum cooperation with only a minimum of coercive pressure."

Ian blanked out again.

"Hmm," the dragon said, moving uncomfortably close to peer at him. "Doesn't take much to shut you down, does it?"

Shaking his head to clear it, Ian frowned. "To be fair, it's late, and I haven't eaten well, and I have never had a dragon in my bedroom before. If I get out of bed nice and slow, you won't, you know, shoot flames at me or anything, will you?"

The dragon snorted. "Of course not. How barbaric. Besides, it would ruin your drapes."

"Right." Ian slid out slowly from underneath the covers, using the time to study the creature in the moonlight. It was much bigger than Ian: its body was almost the size of a mini-van, and it had a long tail that extended out of the bedroom and into the hallway. Its head brushed the ceiling.

He looked closer. As big as the dragon was, Ian felt that there was something . . . odd about it. Sure, the back legs looked like they could knock a tree over with a single kick. The jaws probably contained a lot of sharp teeth. It looked like it might have big wings. Yet, somehow, the whole picture was less menacing than it should have been. It was as though the dragon was missing that rip-your-guts-out-and-chortle-over-a-pile-of-gold edge.

"I'm going to turn on the light, okay?"

"Fine, fine."

The dragon blinked as the lamp flared on. Maybe it was the eyes, Ian thought, now that he could see them clearly. Rather than being beady or penetrating, they were wide and almost . . . *cute*. And the dragon's colour! Sort of a reddish-pink hue with green outlining the edge of each scale. How strange . . .

Ian sat on the edge of the bed. "Okay, for the moment, I'll pretend there is a dragon in my house. Obviously, this is my subconscious trying to tell me something. Let's analyze this."

"This isn't going to involve a couch, is it? I've been waiting forever for you to wake up as it is."

"No couches. What's your name? Perhaps that will give me a clue."

The dragon puffed itself up. "My name is Banebringer Talonsharp of the Grey Terror."

Ian's eyes looked up and down the length of the dragon, taking in all of its pink glory. "Er, really?"

The dragon drooped. "No." It sighed. "Not really."

"So, what is it?"

"Ethmumble Mumblegon."

"What?"

"Mumblether Punmumble."

"Speak up! I can't hear you."

"Ether Pundragon."

"Ether?! What kind of name is that for a dragon?" Ian sat back a little. "This could have serious psychological ramifications."

"You have *no* idea."

"Okay, so your name is Ether. Not a super dragony name, but you must do dragony things?"

"Define 'dragony'," Ether said.

"Hoarding gold."

"Nope."

"Scaring dwarfs?"

"Nuh-uh."

"Chewing up princesses? Battling knights-errant?"

"No princesses . . . especially the ones wearing paper bags. And ixnay on the battles with knights."

"Why?"

Ether studied the ceiling with great care. "Mumblesickmumble."

"Come again?"

"Sightmumblemumble."

"What?"

"Oh for Pete's sake! If you must know, the sight of blood makes me feel nauseous!"

Ian smacked his forehead. "Great. Just great. I have

conjured up a queasy pink dragon named Ether. I must be having a nervous breakdown."

"That's *hot* pink to you, buster."

But Ian wasn't listening. "My career is down the tubes, I am broke, my house hates me, and I am talking to an imaginary dysfunctional dragon. Unless . . . unless this is a hallucination because I thumped my head in the accident this morning . . . Yes, that sounds way better than a nervous breakdown. Still not sure how I'm going to explain this to a doctor though. How embarrassing."

The dragon rolled its eyes. "Oh, get over yourself."

"Eh?"

"Do you have *any* idea how hard it is to seem ferocious when you're this colour? How difficult it is to impress the female dragons when your name is Ether? And I certainly never get invited to join in any dragon games. All because some auth—"

"Uh, do you want that couch?"

"Not at all. I'm just trying to tell you that there are worse situations than yours. I know there are worse than mine." Ether crouched down, putting his head in his front claws. With his dragon back end in the air, he was almost adorable. "And furthermore, I'm not imaginary. I'm real. At least, as far as you're concerned. You've got to believe me."

"Okay, subconscious, why is it so important I believe I have a real dragon in my bedroom?"

Ether assumed a scholarly look and a false German accent. "Because I feel zat vee vill not make any progress until you achcept zee reality of your zituation."

Ian covered his face with his hands. "Oh God. Now it's a queasy pink dragon named Ether that does bad Freud impressions."

"Hot pink. *Hot* pink!" Ether said. "Hey, you brought up the couch. Fine. It looks like we're going to have to go through the whole touch-me-on-the-nose bit."

"You want me to . . . touch your nose?"

"You must have seen or read this somewhere. You have to touch me on the nose to prove to yourself that I'm real."

Ian paused. He checked the dragon's expression, looking for a trap or some kind of joke. Even though it was now technically Tuesday, he wasn't entirely sure Monday was done with him yet.

Ether looked bored and started casually examining a chipped talon. "Go on," he said. "We haven't got all night. I promise I won't bite. I generally swallow people whole."

Ian paled.

"I'm *kidding*." The dragon sighed. "Look, seriously . . . if I had wanted to eat you, I would have done so long before now. You were asleep when I came in, remember?"

The dragon had a point. Ian leaned forward and squared his shoulders. He placed a hand on the dragon's nose. It was warm, and hard, and smooth.

Ian passed out again.

\* \* \*

When Ian came to, Ether was drumming his claws on the floor and attempting to whistle. Since dragon lips did not appear to be built for whistling, he sounded ridiculous.

"I wouldn't have pegged you as a fainter."

"I'm not," Ian said, "under normal circumstances."

"Well, I would hardly expect you to go around fainting under *normal* circumstances."

"No, no," Ian said irritably. "I mean, I've never fainted

before, even in scary situations, and I've been in a few. But apparently, the sight of you is more than I can handle."

"Really?" Ether looked pleased.

"I guess."

"Cool." Now Ether looked doubtful. "Did I use that word right?"

"Now, hang on a minute. Let's agree that you're real. Where are you from, anyway? All the dragons I've, er, well, read about don't go around saying things like 'cool' and doing Freud impressions."

The dragon coiled his tail and brought the tip of it around to scratch a spot behind his ear. "I bet most dragons you've read about aren't named Ether either. For now, I'll say that I'm from another dimension or plane of existence. There's a group of us that's been studying your, er, plane for a while. I'm in charge of the study, so I've been picking up a lot of your expressions."

"You're studying us?" Ian said while reaching for the water bottle he kept on his night table. He took a swig. It tasted real enough. "How? Abductions? Experimentation? Are you planning on invading?"

"Paranoid much?" Ether laughed. "I'm a dragon, not an alien. Without getting too technical, we've been observing you through rift conduits between our two worlds. I really shouldn't say much more in case it goes against your prime corrective."

Ian had to think about this for a minute. "Did you mean prime directive?"

"Yeah, that."

"But that's not re—" Ian began and shook his head. "Never mind. Why are you here?"

Ether looked away uncomfortably and scratched behind his other ear. "Mumblefellmumble."

"Don't start that again."

"Okay, okay. I fell through a rift. I opened one in the wrong place and was trying to look around to see where it was so I could recalculate. I leaned out too far and fell through."

"Where was this rift?"

"About fourteen thousand feet straight up."

"Ouch."

"You're not kidding."

"Not to be morbid or anything, but how come you're not a dragon-shaped crop circle right about now?"

Ether looked back at his wings. "It was a near thing. I was in freefall for what seemed like forever, but I did manage to get the right way up and my wings out. Unfortunately, I lost something in the turbulence. Aaaaannd that's where you come in." Ether lifted a wing gently. There was a large patch of skin showing underneath. It looked raw and painful, not to mention soft and vulnerable.

Ian moved closer. "It looks like you're missing a . . . scale."

The light dawned.

"You're the one who nearly got me killed this morning!" Ian exclaimed. "Or wait . . . Does this mean I've been hallucinating *all day*? Did that tap that went flying actually hit me on the head?" He brought his hands to his cheeks. "Oh God! Does that mean I hallucinated that entire council meeting? And I still have to attend it again in real life? Gaaaah. I can't even hallucinate right! Other people get beaches, or heaven, or . . ."

"We're past that, remember? I'm real," Ether replied. "Anyway, yes. Sorry about that. I couldn't find where the scale had fallen until you had your little adventure. I heard your tire blow. I went looking for the scale afterward, but it was gone."

Ian resisted the urge to stroke the sore spot. "That looks like it hurt."

"Ever bent back your fingernail? Or had one ripped off by accident?"

"Sure."

"Multiply that by a hundred."

"Ow," Ian said, shuddering. "*Ow.*"

Ether looked at the bare spot once more before closing his wing over it protectively. "This will eventually grow back, but in the meantime, I have to go home. I need the old scale and something to hold it in place. And, of course, someone to help me put it back. Otherwise, the trip home is going to be super painful."

"Good grief! How on earth am I supposed to reattach a scale?"

"If I knew the answer to that, I wouldn't be here. I'm an anthropologist, not a doctor."

"You'd think this would be kind of important information for a dragon to know."

"Not really." Ether shrugged. "Like I said, normally, I'd just let it grow back. Any ideas?"

"Hmm," Ian said, not quite believing he was having this conversation. "Staple gun?"

"What's that?"

Ian gave him a brief explanation. A pair of dragon eyebrows shot upward.

"Are you crazy?! How would you like it if I offered to use a staple gun on you?"

"A thought, Ether. A suggestion. Relax."

"Mumblestaplemumblebutt."

"What?!"

"Nothing," said Ether pleasantly. "Just a thought."

"I'll bet," Ian said. "Could we tie it on? With rope?"

"Too much turbulence in the rift conduit. That's why I need the scale back in the first place. And the rope would have to be tied super tight or it would come off and strangle me or something."

"What if—and this is only a suggestion—we were to drill holes at the edge of the scale, and a set of holes near the top of an attached scale, and tie it on that way?"

Ether shook his head almost immediately. "Updrafts."

"What about holes in—"

"Downdrafts."

"What about packing tape? I can never open my grand-mum's packages from England. And if you say sideways drafts, I will thump you on the nose."

"I lost the scale in the first place because of the wind. It's a rough ride, and I doubt tape will hold. Even if we were to have your grandmum pack it." Ether puffed out his cheeks in frustration, making Ian nervous enough to glance at the curtains. "I need to seal my scale edges right down."

"Sealant!" Ian exclaimed. "Will silicone stick?"

"I have no idea."

"Well, what's dragon scale made out of?"

Ether opened his mouth and then shut it again. "Erm, smaller bits of dragon?"

"You don't know what you're made of?"

"I don't even know where I come from. How am I supposed to know what I'm made of?"

"I know what I'm made of, but I don't know where people come from." Ian paused. "Generally speaking, I mean. Like, I know where babies come from. I just . . . I don't know where people come *from*. Generally," he finished, blushing a little.

"Really?" Ether watched his discomfiture with amuse-ment. "You mean you understand the mechanics of how you personally got here, but the origins of humanity aren't known to you."

"Yes," Ian said with relief, tugging at his pyjama collar a little. "That's it."

"So, what are you made out of?"

"Well, on one level, muscle, skin, tissue—"

"Gesundheit."

"—blood and bones. At the atomic level, carbon, oxygen, water, and so on."

From out of nowhere, Ether whipped out a notebook and an overlarge pencil. "Carbon, you say?" he muttered almost to himself. "That may apply to us too . . ."

Ian looked at Ether suspiciously. "There's more than just a rift conduit connecting our two worlds, isn't there? There's a bigger connection."

Ether looked up from his pad, startled. "Maaaaybe." He hesitated. "I'm not sure how much I should tell you, though."

"Why? Because it will alter the space–time continuum or something?"

"Um, sure. Yes, that's it." The pencil started moving surreptitiously.

"That's 'continuum' . . . with two letter 'u's."

The dragon looked sheepish. "Thanks. The truth is, I don't know. I don't even know what the effect of my being here right now is going to be. That's why I'd like to get out of here as quickly as possible."

"Well," Ian said, clapping his hands. "You're going to have to wait until I can get to the hardware store tomorrow morning. I'll need some inspiration. For now, I'm going to bed."

"Can I ask you just one more favour?"

"Sure . . . why not?"

"Do you have anything to eat? I haven't had anything in nearly a day."

"Oh." Ian thought about it. "I have pizza, a leftover pork chop, eggs, some cake, and orange juice. I can't remember what's in the cupboard. What would you like?"

"You mean I have to choose?"

Ian threw his hands in the air. "Yes. No. I don't know. That is way more than I can deal with right now. Help yourself."

\* \* \*

When the alarm went off the next morning, Ian lay in bed for a moment, rubbing his stomach. He was tired from the weird dream he'd had and was feeling slightly woozy. But at least it wasn't Monday anymore.

Then he heard the sound of tin cans being knocked over. A *lot* of tin cans.

Ian staggered downstairs and gasped. The kitchen was a disaster area. There were empty cans all over the floor, discarded wrappers on the counter, boxes in the sink, and dirty dishes on the stove. "W-what have you done?!"

Ether jumped and turned around. "Oh, good morning." The dragon shuffled to look around. "Sorry about the mess. I wasn't sure what to do with all this stuff. Our containers just sort of degrade away when you're done with them. How long do you have to let them lie there?"

"You're not supposed to let them lie around. You have to put them in the garbage."

"Ah," said the dragon. "And then what?"

"You put the garbage outside, and someone comes and takes it away to the landfill."

"And then what happens?"

"Uh, nothing."

"You mean you just let them lie around?"

"Yes, but the point is," Ian said, reaching desperately, "the point is, it's not lying around *here*."

"Hmm. I see." Out came the notebook.

Ian waded through the debris and opened the fridge. Nothing. He checked the freezer. Nada. He opened the cupboard. Empty. "What did you do? Lick them clean?"

Ether hurried over to peer in the cupboard. "Why? Did I miss something?"

"No! There's nothing left! You've cleaned me out!" He closed the cupboard door. "What am I supposed to eat for breakfast?" Ian sagged against the counter. "Where's my coffee?"

Ether looked down at his front claws, where he was grasping the last available can. "There's these peaches," he said, pouting.

"Peaches. Two weeks' worth of groceries have been reduced to peaches."

"That was two weeks' worth? You humans don't eat much."

"Not as much as dragons . . . or so it would seem."

"Well here," Ether said, "let me open this for you." He opened his mouth and drew back his upper lip to expose his two large upper incisors. Looking down his nose, he took careful aim and rammed the can upward onto a tooth.

Ian winced. "I have a can opener for that, you know."

"Weally?" Ether said, twisting the can downward. "Tha wou make thins easiah."

Ian shuddered as the can scraped loose. "I've changed my mind. I'm not hungry."

Ether's face lit up. "Great!" He put his lips to the hole and sucked the peaches out, caving in the sides and crumpling the tin. "Mmm, light syrup."

"I'm going to go have a shower."

"Are you going to that hard store?"

"Hardware. Yes. After I get coffee. Can other people see you, or am I the only one?"

Ether shrugged. "I dunno. I've never been here before."

"Then you'd better stay here."

"You never did tell me your name. What should I call you?"

"Ian. Ian MacDonald."

Ether stuck out a talon. "Pleased to meet you, Ian."

Without thinking, Ian shook the proffered claw. Then he realized how absurd the situation was and pulled back. "Shower. Coffee. Don't eat my furniture."

Ether sighed and peered into the can. "Then maybe you should get some more of these."

\* \* \*

Ian finished his shower, pulled on a pair of jeans and a rugby shirt, and pounded down the stairs. The finial on the last newel post came loose in his hand as he swung off the last step, nearly sending him careening into a wall.

He looked at the wooden decoration and felt a combination of anger and depression wash over him. Everything. Everything seemed broken, and he had absolutely no idea how to begin to fix it.

He took a deep breath to steady himself, chucked the piece of wood onto the chair in the living room, and added it to his mental repair list. He ducked outside and pulled the door closed quickly yet casually, certain that Mrs. Wilson would be keeping an eye on him from across the street. Somehow.

He arrived at the hardware store just as the owner was raising the awnings over the front window.

"Morning, Ian," he said. "You're out bright and early today."

"Morning, Mark."

"What can I help you with?"

He tried to sound normal. "Nothing just yet, thanks. I'll, uh, just take a gander inside. I'll call you if I need you."

"Oh," Mark sounded disappointed.

Ian scuttled into the store and sighed. This was the part he had been dreading. The service could be good in small towns—sometimes too good. Shopkeepers were always eager to help you, to find out what you were buying and why, and it was usually hard to leave the store empty-handed. After all that attention, Ian always felt guilty if he didn't buy something.

He picked an aisle at random and walked down it, looking for ideas. Kitchenware. No luck. Next aisle. Fasteners. Lots of nuts and bolts, but nothing small enough for what he needed. He checked his watch. He should be interrupted right about—

"Any luck?" Mark casually popped around the corner.

"Not yet. Thanks." Ian prayed he would go away.

"Perhaps if you tell me what you're looking for," Mark prompted.

"Well, ah," Ian fumbled, wishing he'd taken the time to come up with a cover story, "I'm looking for something that will stick something to . . . ah . . . something else."

"Is this in your kitchen? Mrs. Wilson said you were having plumbing trouble."

"Ah, no."

"Bathroom?"

"Nope."

"Outdoors?"

"No. Listen, this is a surprise. I really can't say."

"Oh! Who for? Janice?"

"No."

"Tiffany?"

"No."

"Not Melvin and Elinor?"

"I can't say," Ian said, resisting the urge to scream. "You know how it is. Word gets around."

"Sure do. Terrible, isn't it? I always say that the rumours around here travel faster than I do." He laughed. "Say, speaking of Tiffany, did you know that Jamie is going to propose on Saturday night? He's going to take her up to Arlene's for supper and do it right there in the restaurant."

"Does Tiffany know this?"

"Course not. He's been keeping it a secret. He bought the ring yesterday. Jimmy says it's really nice. Now," he said, all business, looking over the shelves. "Would a staple gun do?"

Ian winced and then snickered. "No. What I need has to be able to stick to anything, be super strong, and seal down the edges of my, er, thing, so that the wind can't lift it."

"Why didn't you say so? I have just the thing."

* * *

"Duck tape?"

"No, duct. D-U-C-T."

"And this is going to work, is it?" Ether peered into the box Ian had brought home.

"I hope so. Mark said it was the handyman's secret weapon. Strong, durable, and way better than even grandmum's packing tape. But I can't put it on right now. I'm going to be late for work if I don't get out of here right now."

"Can I come?"

"No. The hardware guy already thinks I'm weird. I can't go around town with a big pin— hot-pink dragon."

"I could hide."

Ian checked him over. "Doubt it. Gotta go. Don't eat anything."

"Nothing *to* eat," Ether muttered.

Ian ran out and hopped in his truck. A few minutes later, he flew through *The Express* front door. The door chimes bingled in his wake.

"Ian!" Janice exclaimed. "What are you doing here?"

Ian stopped in midstride. "I work here?"

"You haven't forgotten about the Agriculture Minister's visit to Frank's farm, have you?"

Of course he had.

"Of course I haven't," Ian said. "I just . . . came back for a fresh notepad." He ran to the supply cupboard and grabbed a pad. "See? Pad," he said and trotted back out to the truck. In a few minutes, he was flying down the road again.

"Who's the babe?"

"Ack!" Ian jumped, and the truck went skidding. He stopped in a shower of gravel and threw it into park.

Ether crawled up into the front seat, which groaned in protest.

"What the heck are you doing here?" Ian demanded. "*How* are you here?"

"Well . . ." Ether folded his tail into his lap. "There are lots of disadvantages to being me. But there's lots of advantages too. One is brains, two is magical abilities, including being able to resize for the occasion." He leaned forward to look in the side mirror. "Three is being good-looking." He smoothed a talon over an eyebrow.

"Ether, you can't come with me. Government officials are going to be there. Bigger newspapers will be sending reporters. Radio and television. It's a press conference. I absolutely cannot have you there."

"Objects," Ether read slowly, "in . . . mirror . . . are . . . closer . . ."

"Are you listening?!"

"Sure, Ian."

"Then I have to take you back to the house."

"What time is this conference?"

"Nine-thirty."

"No time!" Ether happily tapped the dashboard clock. "Unless you drive quickly, we'll be late as it is."

"Ack!" Ian rammed the truck into gear and stomped on the gas pedal.

"So, who's the babe?"

"If you mean Janice, that's my boss."

"What's this do?" Ether reached over and pulled a lever. The windshield wipers came on with a spray of fluid. Ian smacked his claw away, and the truck veered to the right.

"Stop that! You'll get us killed!" Ian said, straightening out.

"She can't be both?" Ether reached for the ashtray and pulled it out.

"What?"

"The boss. She can't be a babe?"

"No," he said and pushed the ashtray back into place. "What era did you drop in from? She's a smart, motivated woman who is also my boss."

"So you haven't noticed how good-looking she is. I mean, for a human."

"No. I mean, yes, I have, but I don't think about her that way. She's my employer."

"Right." Ether touched the radio knob. Static-laced music blared.

"Cut that out!" Ian yelled over the din. He turned off the radio and glanced at Ether suspiciously. "How do you know what she looks like?"

"Saw her through the window," Ether said. "So you have

never, ever thought of her romantically? Out of your league, eh?"

"Hey!" Ian took a deep breath. "I have thought about it, thank you very much. And no, I don't think she's out of my league. Probably. But I don't think it's a good idea to be involved with people you work with. Besides, I'm going to leave here soon, and I don't want to have to break off ties."

"When are you going to go?" Ether twiddled the sun visor.

"As soon as I finish the storyline for my new video game series."

"Really?" Ether looked intrigued. "How long have you been working on this game?"

Ian flushed. "Two years," he muttered.

"Hmmm." Ether nodded. "And how long have you been here?"

"Two years," Ian grated.

"I see."

Ian twisted in his seat to face Ether. "What's *that* supposed to mean?"

"Oh, nothing."

"That sounded like more than nothing. I can hear it in the tone of your voice."

"Well," Ether said, crossing his front claws in his lap and looking airily out the window. "It's just that two years is a long time to be preparing to leave. You're missing out on a lot."

"What would you know about it?"

"Tree."

"Pardon?"

"Tree. Twelve o'clock. Collision."

Ian faced the road again. They were bearing down on a large oak tree at the side of the road. "Ack!" He jerked the steering wheel to the left.

"Has anyone told you that you seem to have a limited vocabulary? That's probably why it's taking you so long to write the story for this game thingy. Perhaps you should socialize more."

"Listen," Ian said through gritted teeth. "I'm working on it. As soon as I've written the storyline and licensed it to a reputable game studio, I'll have enough money to move back to Toronto. It's just taking me longer to . . . work out some of the details . . . than I thought." He stopped for a minute. "I can't believe I'm explaining myself to you."

"That's what guy talk is for, Ian."

"*Guy talk*?!" Ian sputtered. "This is not guy talk. This is a reporter who has finally lost his marbles talking to an imaginary pin— *hot*-pink dragon in the front seat of a dying pickup truck."

"Boy, does that guy ever own a lot of cows."

Ian looked in the rearview mirror. "Argh! That was Frank's place!"

"See? Your vocabulary is improving already!"

Ian glared at Ether and spun the truck around. They bumped and rattled back toward the farm and pulled into Frank's long driveway. There were already lots of cars there, including vehicles from the other media outlets. Ian cursed under his breath. He reached into the back of the cab and pulled out his camera bag. "You," he said distinctly, "will stay here. Don't eat anything. Stay below the window. Or I will run over more than just *one* scale today."

Ether sulked. "Touchy, touchy."

Ian got out of the truck, slammed the door, and began marching toward the barn. A moment later, he marched back. He opened the door, hit the locks, and closed it again.

"Hmph," Ether sniffed.

\* \* \*

Ian made his way into the barn and found Frank chatting amiably with some of his friends. He was wearing grey coveralls, a ball cap, and a pair of battered boots.

"Morning, Ian," he said. "Any sign of the minister?"

"Not that I saw coming in. He's not here yet?"

"Nope. I just hope his staff can find the place with the directions I gave them."

"I'm sure they'll be using GPS if they need it," Ian replied. "What's on the agenda?"

"We're hoping he'll be announcing new coverage policies for the farm insurance program. The Cattleman's Association's been lobbying hard for better protection the past two years."

Ian pulled out his notebook and began writing. "What's your position with the association these days?"

"President of the local group," Frank said, "and a director for the Ontario Association."

Another farmer joined them. "Playing up to the press again, Frank?"

"Matty!" Frank clapped him on the shoulder. "You're just jealous. How's it going?"

"Got everything into the ground on time, so that's something. I just hope we get some rain soon."

"You got that right. Oh yeah, oh yeah," Frank said. "Definitely need some moisture. Say, did you hear the latest about Blake and Robert's wife?"

Matty cleared his throat, casting a significant and completely unsubtle glance in Ian's direction. Frank remembered where he was and looked a bit nervous. "Um, this is off the record, right?"

Ian put on a smile. Everyone assumed that since he was a

reporter, he was likely to print anything they ever said—even the gossip. "Of course," he said, resorting to his stock response, "unless you've got pictures for me."

Frank and Matty laughed. Just then, there was a commotion outside, and a crowd of people moved into the barn. "Looks like he's arrived," said Frank. "Gotta go. Catch me later for a response, Ian."

"Right."

Frank went to go meet the minister. A Halifax lawyer, the minister seemed conspicuously overdressed in a dark blue silk suit and expensive black shoes. Ian knew from the evening news that he was vocal in parliament, with a tendency to shoot from the hip and hit his own two feet every time. The minister kept looking nervously at the ground, as though he expected cow pats to fling themselves directly under his shoes. By the looks of him, he wasn't going to last long in this portfolio. He smiled gamely when Frank approached.

"Minister," Frank said. "Welcome. Let me show you around before we get you set up at the back."

The minister looked helplessly at an assistant, who shrugged. He followed Frank toward the stalls, where one of the animals snorted and stamped a hoof, making him flinch.

While Frank explained the intricacies of cattle farming, Ian moved to the back of the barn, where some hay bales had been stacked in a makeshift stage and podium. Members of the local Ladies' Auxiliary bustled about, setting out coffee and homemade desserts. Having missed breakfast, and being like any other good reporter, Ian staked out a spot near the free-food table and checked his camera.

After about fifteen minutes, Frank finally brought the minister toward the stage. Visibly wilting with relief, the minister sprang onto the hay bales and beamed as he was introduced. He stepped up to the podium and pulled out some notes.

"Fusarium," he began with a flourish, "has been the scourge of this community. It is the hope of this government that . . ."

There were some surprised whispers from the crowd. Ian leaned over to Frank. "What's fusarium?"

"Some kind of disease for melons, I think," Frank replied, looking bewildered. The minister's assistant looked panicked and jumped up on stage. There was a hushed conversation between the two, and the assistant handed over a different set of notes.

The minister turned red, coughed, and started over. "The global beef market is a treacherous place these days . . ."

Ian snapped some photos, got some crowd shots, and returned to his place. Something in the corner of his eye caught his attention, and he turned in time to see a small pink claw reach out from underneath the table toward a piece of pie. He sucked in his breath and quickly looked around to see if anyone else had noticed. The audience seemed focused on the speech.

Ian sidled over to the edge and attempted to bat the claw away. There was an indignant squeak from below, and Ether whacked him back. A flurry of slapping followed, becoming progressively more violent, until Ian accidentally squashed a slice of cheesecake. One of the ladies from the auxiliary turned and glared at him.

"Flies," Ian mouthed at her and made some exaggerated swatting motions over the table. When she finally looked away, Ether swiped the cheesecake. A few seconds later, a piece of apple pie vanished. "Ether!" Ian hissed, prodding under the table with his shoe. "Stop that!" The dragon shoved him away.

" . . . So it is my intention to help put an end to these

unfair market practices!" the minister continued, stabbing the air with a finger for emphasis. The audience applauded, and he warmed to his subject, grinning. "With this new legislation..."

Two more slices disappeared. Desperate, Ian shoved the remaining desserts into the centre of the table. Ether reached up again and patted the empty space. When he couldn't find anything, he balled up his fist and shook it threateningly. The talon disappeared again, and Ian breathed a sigh of relief. He tried to focus on the announcement.

"Tariffs on these and other products will be raised by two and a half percent over the next two years," the minister enthused. The audience applauded some more.

Ian scribbled in his notebook for several minutes until a sound caught his attention. He cocked his head this way and that, trying to determine where it was coming from. The sound became louder and more frequent. Growing alarmed —and suspicious—he pretended to drop his pencil so he could check under the table.

Ether, now the size of a large dog, looked back. His legs were splayed out in front of him, and his tail stuck straight out the back. He had both claws clamped tightly over his muzzle, and his eyes were wide. "*Hic!*" he said, bouncing a little. "*Hic!*"

Ian grabbed his pencil and straightened quickly. One of the television people gave him a quizzical look. He smiled and tried to concentrate on the minister but kept thinking dark thoughts about dragon stew.

Ether's hiccups grew louder. Some of the farmers nearby began to glance at each other and at the cattle. Ian could hear the "hic" followed by a thud as Ether's head hit the underside of the table.

"Are there any questions from the press?" the minister paused. "How about you?" he said, pointing directly at Ian.

"Ah . . ." Ian fumbled, flipping desperately through his notes. "Right, uh . . . how about . . . what guarantee does the government have for us that the legislation will last beyond the next election?"

"Well, of course that's because the government will still be there after the next election, am I right?" The crowd laughed. Ian took the opportunity to aim a sharp kick backward under the table.

"*Hic–ack!*"

Everyone turned to face him again. Forced to go on the offensive, he immediately turned and glared at the woman from the auxiliary. As everyone followed his gaze, she gasped and turned red, totally bemused. But the minister kept talking, so everyone lost interest. And the hiccups stopped.

The event broke up at last. Frank gave Ian a quote and moved to help the ladies pass out coffee. The minister worked the room, getting closer and closer to the exit. He was just about to leave when someone smelled smoke.

"Fire! Fire in the hay bales!"

* * *

"Are you still going to help me?" Ether asked quietly about halfway into town.

"You came in when I asked you not to, ate half the desserts, got a loud case of the hiccups, started a fire, and you're still asking me about help?"

"I didn't start the fire!" Ether protested. "I didn't light it! I tried to fight it."

"Right. Cattle barns are known for spontaneous combustion."

"Honest, Ian, it wasn't me. It couldn't have been."

"It just so happens that a dragon was in the barn the same day it was incinerated."

Ether rolled his eyes. "Please. They got it out before it even touched the walls. And it *wasn't* me. I think someone dropped something. What do you call those long tube things that people burn in their mouths? They're like personal smokestacks or something."

"Cigarettes? You're telling me someone dropped a cigarette?"

"I think so. One of the minister's entourage."

Ian snorted. "Good cover story." They rode in silence for a while. Then Ian said, "First, I'm going to drop you off at the house. Then I'm going to work. If you stay put, and if you can stop eating long enough for me to regain my temper, I might consider not turning you in to the zoo."

"Oh."

They got to the house, and Ether wisely disappeared inside without protest. Ian returned to *The Express* and found the building empty, save for Janice.

"Lunchtime," Janice said by way of explanation. "How bad was the fire?"

Ian was not surprised that she'd heard already. "Not very. Frank lost a few bales before they got extinguishers on it. You know most of those guys are volunteer firefighters anyway." He gave her a rundown of the event. "I got pictures of all of it."

"Good," Janice said. She hesitated. "Say, are you okay?"

Ian suppressed an urge to groan. "Never better, why?"

"It's just that someone said you were acting kind of funny at the conference—"

"Ah. Just hungry. Missed breakfast."

"And talking to yourself in the truck?"

Ian made a mental note to start doing everything under

cover of darkness. He forced a laugh. "No one has ever heard of hands-free phone calls in this town?"

"Of course, of course," Janice said. "It's just you seemed rattled when you came in this morning, and when I heard that too . . . well, I thought I'd check to see if everything was okay. You've been quite reliable, but you don't share much about yourself, and I . . ." she paused, looking strangely embarrassed, " . . . that is to say, *we* were a bit concerned."

"I promise not to skip breakfast ever again."

Janice laughed. "Fair enough. Give me a write-up on the conference and a sidebar about the fire."

"On it," Ian said and escaped to his desk.

* * *

Ian did some shopping before coming home. When he stepped into his living room with several bags of groceries, he found Ether watching television.

"What have you eaten?"

"Nothing, I swear." He chewed on his nails nervously. "Are you still mad at me?"

"I haven't called the zoo. Yet."

"I'm really sorry, Ian. I don't know what came over me."

"Your stomach?" Ian suggested.

"Well, yes. I guess so. Those desserts smelled so good."

Ian worked his fingers loose from the handles of the grocery bags before setting them down on the floor. "On that we can agree. Why on earth did you even come along today? You couldn't have known there would be food."

Ether shrugged sadly. "Curiosity, I guess. I only get to observe this world through the rifts for short periods of time. I was hoping some real live experiences would teach me more than second-hand observations. Besides, it seemed like it would be fun. It's one of those once-in-a-lifetime things, you know?" Ether sniffed loudly, picked up his tail, and began wringing it. "I've been thinking about this all afternoon, and I feel terrible. I really hope I haven't done you any harm, Ian. I didn't mean it."

Ian watched incredulously as Ether's eyes puddled up. "Oh, for God's sake," Ian said. "Don't start crying on me."

"I'd never forgive myself if you got into trouble because of me."

"I'm not in trouble," Ian said, feeling horrible for being so grouchy all day. "The folks in town think I'm a bit weird, that's all. No harm done."

"Really?"

"Really," Ian said and took the groceries into the kitchen. There was a loud honking noise that sounded like Ether blowing his nose. When Ian returned to the living room, the drapes were swaying suspiciously. Ian decided he didn't want to know.

"Thank you, Ian," Ether said, dabbing his eyes with the end of his tail.

"Here," Ian said gruffly, handing him a can. "I brought you these."

"Peaches!" Ether brightened immediately. "I don't know what to say."

"For the sake of my nerves, how about 'pass the can opener'? I'm not sure I can handle you levering it open with your teeth again." Ian handed him the tool and indicated the television. "What have you been watching?"

Ether opened the can and savoured the fruit before answering. "I'm not sure. On one channel, there's nothing but people jumping around with musical instruments and doing things that seem to have nothing to do with the song they're singing. On another channel, they seem to be having a storytelling contest. Some people sit on a stage, and the audience laughs, or cries, or boos them."

Ian nodded. "Music videos and talk shows. Welcome to daytime television. I'd tell you not to think of them as an accurate reflection of society, but I don't know how true that is really."

"Do you have the duck tape?"

"Duct. Yes. What do we need to do after I get the scale back on you?"

Ether thought for a moment. "I need to go somewhere where I can create a rift conduit. I'll need more space than this." He spread his claws to point to the living room.

"Okay," Ian said. "I'll pack a flashlight and the tape and take you to a fallow field out of town when it's dark. But first, supper."

Ether grinned. "That sounds good to me."

\* \* \*

Ian had just put a pot of water on to boil for pasta when his phone rang. The screen read *Disgruntled Robot Studios*.

"Omigod, omigod, omigod!" Ian put a hand to his forehead. He had almost completely forgotten he'd put an application in when they'd advertised a story developer position there a few weeks ago. He peeked out at Ether to make sure he was occupied and not likely to interrupt. The dragon seemed thoroughly entranced by something on TV; it sounded like one of David Attenborough's wildlife documentaries. Ian took a deep breath and tried not to visualize himself happily saying yes to a job offer, packing everything into a moving van, and heading back to Toronto. Too much to hope for.

Ian thumbed the answer icon. "Hello?"

"Is this Ian MacDonald?"

"Speaking."

"I'm Suparna Jain, and I do talent acquisition for Disgruntled. We have your application, and we'd like you to come in for an interview if you're still interested in pursuing the position."

"Oh good," Ian said, pumping his fist while trying to sound professional and not at all desperately keen. "Yes, I am. What times do you have available, and is there anything I should bring with me?"

"We've got four slots open next week and two the next. The format will be a panel interview and then a pitch session, so bring your best idea. We'll be looking for something that has franchise potential."

Ian's heart sank. The job listing had made it sound as if the developer would be taking over existing storylines, not coming up with new ones. He'd put his name in because he'd thought it would help him get his creative juices flowing again while providing a higher salary.

"Great," he said gamely. "How about those times the following week?"

They finalized the interview time, and he rang off. He pressed his fist to the bridge of his nose, not sure why he'd just agreed to go see them. It would mean using up a sick day at work, paying for a train ticket—no way was he trusting the truck to get him to Toronto and back—and he didn't have any idea what to pitch them. The pitch would almost certainly be a disaster. And, if he thought about it, was he especially eager to give another company whatever he *did* manage to come up with, only to be screwed over and terminated in the next big merger or bankruptcy?

And yet . . . he wasn't sure he could face another early morning council meeting.

A bit of boiling water splashed out of the pot onto the burner and hissed away into steam. He turned down the water and poured in the macaroni, hoping he'd come up with something—anything—in time for the interview.

\* \* \*

They snuck outside at eleven that night. This time, Ian noticed that when Ether got in the passenger side, the truck suspension dipped and the springs creaked in annoyance. He realized that Ether's weight must be the same, even though he was smaller, and wondered how that must work. Ian pushed the door closed as quietly as he could. Ether flinched.

"Watch the tail!"

"Sorry," Ian hissed into the darkness. He got into the cab and started the truck. The engine sounded abnormally loud in the stillness of the night.

They drove until Ian found a quiet spot several kilometres out of town. Ether looked around and nodded in satisfaction. "This will be just fine."

It took Ian several minutes to tape the scale in place, working as he was with a ticklish dragon and very little light. Finally, after some test moves and stretches, Ether nodded his approval.

He paced out a large circle and checked the sky. He made some vague gestures and paced the circle again. "Carry the one, add two . . ." he muttered. He stuck a claw in his mouth and held it up in the air to test the breeze. Then he cracked his knuckles one by one and started doing elaborate stretches.

Finally, Ian couldn't stand it any longer. "Will you get on with it?!"

"Oh, all right," Ether said and snapped his talons. There was a loud popping noise, followed by a long, low hissing sound. A bright circle of light appeared in front of the dragon. The hair on the back of Ian's neck stood up with an electrical charge.

"That's it?"

"I was trying to be more impressive, but you weren't having it," Ether grumbled.

Ian stepped closer to the light. The circle had widened. It now looked like a large, round doorway. Peering through it, Ian could make out trees and a pleasant-looking meadow. "That's home, huh? It looks a lot like here."

"It has to," Ether remarked. "Well, I guess this is goodbye."

The phrase startled Ian. He wasn't sure what he'd been expecting. Perhaps a sudden reveal that Ether was some sort of soap-making alter ego or something. Or that he'd come to and find himself on his kitchen floor, concussed but full of dragony wisdom from a really good dream. But the air seemed quite chilly and real, the rift conduit sizzled loudly, and he was wide awake.

"I suppose it is," Ian said slowly. "Um, well, the next time you miscalculate a rift, let me know in advance so I can lay on a supply of tape and canned fruit."

Ether smiled. "I will." There was an awkward pause. He cleared his throat and waved. "Goodbye."

Ian waved back. "Right. Goodbye."

Ether turned around and jumped through the circle of light. There was a flash, and he was gone.

Ian was alone in the field, with nothing but the frogs singing in the nearby creek for company.

The frogs were super loud.

The circle seemed to be shrinking. Ian glanced back at his truck and looked at the light again. He thought about going back to his lonely house, and his pile of bills, and his blank computer screen. A very blank screen.

A land that included dragons, Ian decided, would probably be quite inspirational.

All he needed was one idea...

The circle shrank some more.

He ran to the truck, grabbed a notebook and pencil, and pelted back to the rift conduit. Before he could talk himself out of it, he jumped through.

PART II

*S*omewhere in the sky, a low whistle pierced the air. It got louder and louder, and the pitch got higher and higher.

It was accompanied by another lower but considerably louder tone that sounded something like:

"AAAAAAAAAAAAAAAGGGGGGGGHHHHHHHHH—"

ALL OVER THE MEADOW BELOW, little animals stopped what they were doing and looked up. A dark spot in the sky started to swell.

A small crowd gathered near the estimated point of impact. "Say," a rabbit nudged his companion, "is that a bird?"

"Nah," said the other rabbit. "I think it's some sort of plane."

"Bets on where it lands?" a field mouse asked.

"Three carrots says it'll land in the trees," the first rabbit said.

"A pile of seed, and it's heading for the open space on the hill," a blue jay chirped.

"No way," the mouse replied. "I'll bet four walnuts it'll land in the water."

"Deal!" everyone said and looked up again.

The dark shape plunged downward and vanished into the treetops in a fluttery explosion of leaves. There was the sound of something soft hitting wood.

"I win!" the rabbit exclaimed.

"Wait," the blue jay said, cocking his head and holding up a wing. "I don't think it's finished."

As one, the crowd leaned forward to listen. Timber creaked, softly at first and then more loudly. This was followed by a loud *craack!* and more sounds of something soft hitting wood many times. The trees bounced and shook. There was a *thud*, and the dark shape appeared at the edge of the woods. It rolled to the crest of the hill and then . . . teetered on the edge and disappeared. There were several loud *thumpeta thumpeta* noises, followed by a *whompf* and, finally, a distant splash.

"How do you like that?" the mouse said.

There was an inarticulate shout of rage in the distance.

"I still won," insisted the rabbit. "It hit the trees first."

The shouting became louder and more coherent. One sounded distinctly like "*. . . hurt that dragon!*"

"Yes, but it went through that open space on the hill after that," the blue jay said.

"*. . . pluck out all his scales . . .*"

"But it *stopped* in the water," the mouse said. "So, you're both wrong. I win."

"*. . . hang him up by the tail . . .*"

"It's just like you to worm out of a bet," the rabbit said accusingly. "You did this last week too."

"*. . . drag him behind the truck . . .*"

"That's entirely different. We had to call that off on account of rain." The mouse quivered indignantly. "Now, pay up. I won the bet."

"Um . . . guys? Take a look," the blue jay said.

They stopped arguing and gasped. A man towered above them. He was dripping wet, covered in mud, and plastered in leaves. His chest heaved.

"I'm gonna kill him," he said.

Just then, Ether Pundragon flew over and landed beside the animals. "Hey, gang. Everything okay? I heard shouting. What's—" He looked at Ian. "Oh, *bother*."

\* \* \*

"How was I supposed to know you were going to follow me?" Ether grumped.

"You left the door open, for Pete's sake. What did you think I was going to do? I thought you said you'd been studying humans."

"I had no idea that the rift stayed open."

"And what kind of an idiot puts a rift in the sky anyhow?"

Ether sighed. "You're being unreasonable, Ian."

"I was falling for thirty minutes!" Ian shouted. He took a deep breath. "I'm being *quite* reasonable under the circumstances." He paused to look around. "Where are we going anyhow?"

They were walking through beautiful, sunlit woods, with Ether leading the way. "I'm trying to find a conveniently abandoned hunter's lodge. Or a cabin. We need to get you dried off and warmed up. There's usually one around in situations like this."

"What? When people just drop out of the sky like a rock? How many times does this happen anyway?!"

"No, no." Ether shook his big head. "When someone is trudging through the woods, wet, cold, wounded, etcetera and in need of shelter. Something always comes up, but not until that someone starts to despair. Are you despairing yet?"

"I'm despairing of ever being sane again," Ian replied.

"Try harder."

They kept walking. Ian peered through the trees, hoping to find the cabin in question. A flower smiled at him.

He stopped.

"Um, Ether? Is this normal?"

Ether turned around. "Is what normal?"

"This flower. It's . . . smiling at me."

Ether trotted back to see. "Oh, of course. Those are twolips. Make a tea out of those, they perk you right up."

Ian nodded as though that made perfect sense. "And what

about these?" He pointed to a fruit bush. All the little berries had tiny white beards.

"Elderberries. Good for stiff joints. Those flowers beside them? Foxgloves. Good for when you're feeling embarrassed."

"Embarrassed?"

"Yes. They're for covering up faux pas."

Ian buried his face in his hands. "Wonderful. I have arrived in the Land of Excruciatingly Bad Puns."

"No," said Ether in all seriousness, "but that could be west of here. I'd have to look at a map."

"I could really use that cabin now, Ether."

"Oh good." Ether grinned. "That means it should be in the next clearing."

They walked for a few more minutes. Sure enough, there was a cabin where the trees thinned out. They went in, Ether instantaneously changing size to be able to fit through the door. It was a one-room cabin with a single dirty window and a door. In the dim light, Ian could make out a rough-hewn table and chair, a bed frame, a chest, and what looked like a pantry cabinet. One small wall was taken up by a fire-place. Ian could smell damp ash.

Ether was rifling through the pantry. "There'll be clothes in the chest. You hungry? There's lots of jerky in here. Oooh, and tea! Tea fixes everything. Lemme see if I can get a fire going."

Ian opened the heavy wooden chest. Inside, he found a pair of soft leather boots, a pair of dark green trousers, a brown tunic, and a belt with a small dagger and scabbard attached. With his back to the dragon, he quickly and self-consciously changed out of his wet clothing and into the new material. By the time he transferred the contents of his pockets and turned around again, Ether had a fire going in the stone hearth and was rummaging in the pantry again. He emerged triumphant, brandishing a small cast-iron kettle. "Say," he said, glancing at Ian. "Looks pretty good on you."

"Thanks." Ian smoothed down the sleeves of his tunic. "It's almost as though it was made for me; it fits so well."

"Mmmhmm," Ether said. He pulled the lid of the kettle and held it up to the light, squinting at the inside. "Looks cleanish. Check the trunk again, will you? There'll likely be a skin full of water and maybe, if you're lucky, a gourd of ale for later."

Ian returned to the chest and found both. "That's weird. Just as you said. Have you been here before?"

"Not here specifically," Ether answered, "but in this situation. I told you there's always a stash of supplies when you need it. Clothing, non-perishable food, a decent weapon . . . that sort of thing."

"And these stashes appear out of nowhere?"

"Only when your situation appears hopeless, or desperate, or something. It's supposed to give you enough to carry on."

"I still don't understa—"

Suddenly, an arrow whizzed in through the open door. It sliced through the air, passed Ian's ear, and landed with a dramatic thwack in the wall. The free end of the arrow vibrated with a distinctive *tuuuuunnnng* noise.

Ether heaved a deep sigh. "I really hate Questing Season."

"We're under attack!" Ian exclaimed.

"Relax," Ether said. "It's me they're after."

"But that nearly hit me!"

"Some have better aim than others." Ether stood up and stuck his head out the door. "You!" he shouted. "You with the crossbow. Knock it off!"

"Hark!" came the reply. "Yonder magical beast bellows with ire; be not afraid, my stalwart comrades!"

"Great," Ether muttered. "Purists." He cleared his throat

and declaimed, "Come forward, thou snivelling cowards and showest me your miserable visages! Come forward, or I will smite thee where thou standest!"

"Standest?" Ian asked.

"I'm a little rusty," Ether whispered. "C'mon. They won't shoot while we parley."

Ether and Ian went outside. One by one, people emerged from the woods. Ian counted four . . . dwarfs? And then there was another creature that was much shorter again, and two humans. They were dressed in torn leather jerkins, mismatched bits of armour, and battered boots. Two of them were plainly terrified. The rest just looked pathetic.

"What ho!" a dwarf with an overlarge helmet stepped forward. "We hast answered your challenge, evil wyrm. Takest your best shot!"

"No can do," Ether said.

"Hark! Thou art admitting thou art a recreant? A poltroon?" The dwarf shook his sword so hard his helmet slipped over his eyes. He hastily shoved it back. "Methinks thee the snivelling coward!"

"Noooo," Ether said and produced a piece of paper. "But I have been removed from the Approved Questing Season Targets Index. I'm protected."

"Thou art?"

"I is." Ether waved the paper. "By order of the council. See for yourself."

The dwarf waddled over and took the paper. "Nuts," he mumbled. "How are we supposed to level up?" Ether raised a sardonic eyebrow. "I mean," the dwarf fumbled, "I mean fie. Yes, fie! Curses! Woe to us! We art doomed! Our mighty quest is a failure!"

"Don't overdo it," Ether advised.

"Sorry," the dwarf said and blushed. "Um, knowest thou of another worthy task?" He lowered his voice a little.

"Something not too tough? I mean," he gestured furtively at his companions, "we're not exactly rolling twenties here."

"Well," Ether said, thinking quickly, "I've heard rumours of giant spiders in these parts."

"Spiders!" one of the other dwarfs squeaked. His companion kicked him.

The leader of the party looked thoughtful. "Spiders, you say? Evil arachnids? Dark creatures of the night?"

"Very dark and terribly evil," Ether assured him and waxed eloquent. "The last traveller I spoke to talked of a vast horde deep in the forest. Poor devil, he was lucky to escape. The rest of his friends hang suspended from the trees in little webby bundles, with nothing but a nose, a patch of beard, or a small piece of their hood sticking out. He fears the loathsome creatures will eat his fellows alive."

The squeaky dwarf passed out. One of the humans stuck his hands deep in his pockets and sulked. "This is why I live where the air hurts my face."

The leader glared at them both. "We shall pursue these vile insects with *all* of our strength," he said. He turned back to Ether. "Which way?"

Ether chose a direction and pointed. "Ho!" said the dwarf, and he led his ragtag band of adventurers back into the trees.

The dragon watched them go. "They get more newbie by the year, I swear."

Ian gave Ether a dubious look. "Giant spiders? Little webbed bundles of dwarfs? Questers and abandoned cabins full of supplies? Why does that all sound so familiar?"

Ether shrugged. "You probably read it someplace."

"Where *are* we?"

Ether headed back into the cabin. "Didn't I tell you already? Sorry. Welcome to the Connectome."

\* \* \*

IT WAS GETTING DARK, and the fire cast pleasant shadows against the wall behind them. Ether had found a thick wool blanket under the bed, and they'd spread it out in front of, but not too close to, the hearth. The jerky was surprisingly decent and a good counterpoint to the slightly bitter tea.

"Okay," Ian said around a mouthful of food. "Start over from the beginning." Ether had decided that since both of them had inadvertently visited each other's worlds and nothing had broken, providing some background information likely wouldn't hurt either.

"Well," Ether said. "It's still all theoretical at the moment. But as far as we can tell, everything in the Connectome is a product of the human imagination."

"But I thought you told me that you were real?"

"Don't interrupt, I'm getting to that."

"Sorry. It's just that I got stuck on that the first time through."

Ether stretched. "Fine. Maybe if I gave you a specific example . . . something less abstract?"

Ian wondered what could be less abstract than nearly getting shot by a crossbow bolt or whatever that had been, but he nodded anyway.

Ether stretched out on his stomach, braced his elbows on the ground, and propped his chin up on his front claws. "Let's say you wrote a short story or something, and the main character was this really gorgeous dragon named Ginger. She's long and sleek, a beautiful proper dragon-red colour, proud eyes, and a really great set of—"

"Ether!"

"—wings," Ether finished. "What did you think I was going to say?"

"Never mind."

"Well, anyway," the dragon continued, "let's also say that you got this short story published. Naturally, since Ginger is such a babe, the story becomes pretty popular. Lots of people read it. When you read or listen to a story, what you're doing is recreating the author's world in your mind. As more and more people read your story, the Ginger character will get recreated over and over again. Pretty soon, she'll become part of the culture. There will be memes and catchphrases about her, all of which serve to increase her reach. She'll take on a life of her own. At some point—and we don't know the threshold for this—she'll show up here in the Connectome."

"So," Ian said thoughtfully, "what you're saying is this place is a collection of literary characters? Like Merlin, the wizard from the legend of King Arthur?"

"Ol' Merl'? Yeah, he's here. Several different versions of him, in fact. But it's not just things from books. The Connectome has characters from your radio and television. Plenty here from your oral traditions too. You have no idea how many times I've run into a big strong caveman who supposedly took out a mammoth singlehandedly."

"I see." Ian took another bite of jerky.

"It's not just characters either," Ether said, shifting his large pink bottom end to edge it closer to the fire. "Your ideas, myths, musical compositions, theories, poems, games, and even jokes all take physical form here. To paraphrase, anything a human mind can conceive is achieved here."

"I think I'm starting to get it," Ian said. "When you said that you were the product of an author's sick sense of humour, you weren't kidding, were you? Someone back where I live wrote a story with you as a prominent character, didn't they? And enough people have read it for you to appear here."

"By George—whoever he is—I think you're getting it!" Ether nodded approvingly. "Hey, did you ever learn anything about the collective unconscious? It's similar to what I'm talking about."

"I've heard the term but not read about it in any depth, no."

"Darn. I was going to tell you that we're all just Jung at heart here."

"Ether, that was terrible."

"Sorry."

"No, you're not." Ian smiled at him. "Did you just show up here one day, fully formed and punning badly?"

"Not quite. As far as we can tell, we show up first in the Flux, in sort of a ghost or embryonic form, and then become more corporeal as more people become aware of us. At a certain point, we become real enough to pop out and take up residence here. The flip side seems to be true too. If humans forget about us, we start to fade."

Ian paused for some tea and then said, "The Flux?"

"Kind of a permanent rift conduit. Also kind of purgatory or halfway point between our worlds. You can see all kinds of things swirling around in it. Tens of thousands or tens of millions of them. We have no idea how much the Flux holds."

"You need something to measure it. Maybe something like a flux capacitor?"

Ether reached for the kettle, pouted when he saw it was empty, and got up to refill it. "I wish. We have a lot of projects on the go already, though."

"Who's this 'we'?"

"Oh, the Origins Committee. I'm part of this research group looking into where we came from and trying to figure out how it all works." Ether yawned, revealing a mouth full of rather sharp-looking teeth. "That Merlin guy you mentioned? He was the first to discover how to make smaller, less energetic rift conduits. Took him years of studying the Flux. Once we knew how to make them, we began watching your world and discovering connections. We love rifting into movie theatres, library reading rooms, and especially university lectures."

"Why haven't you been spotted before now?"

"Normally, the rifts we make are only big enough to peep through. That one I made in the wrong spot over your town was way too big, which is why I fell through."

"Do you know who created you, Ether?"

"Not yet," Ether replied mournfully. "I've been looking for a long time. But there's just so much to study! You humans are a busy lot. And as you may have noticed, sometimes things don't always come through the Flux without being altered in some way when they're made corporeal. That makes it difficult to figure out what the original was supposed to be."

"That's too bad. I wish I could help, but I can honestly say I've never heard anything about hot-pink dragons before now."

"Maybe you can help. With other stuff, I mean. As long as you're here, I might as well take you on a tour and then introduce you to the other members of the Origins Committee. You might be able to help us trace some other things."

"I'd like that." Ian stretched out on his back, sighing with contentment as he sank down into the soft wool. "There's just one thing I'm still not clear on, though."

"What's that?"

"What kind of form does an idea take here? Or a musical composition?"

"Just about any form is possible. I'll give you an example. Did you ever learn anything about Heisenberg's uncertainty principle?"

"This isn't another setup line, is it? Even you couldn't pun with a name like Heisenberg."

"No, no." Ether grinned. "It's a legitimate question."

"All right." Ian tried to think back to his high school

physics class. "Isn't that the theory that when you get right down to the quantum level of things, the more precisely you measure one property, the less precisely you know the other property?"

"That's right. Often confused with the observer effect. Of course, it's all weird at the quantum level."

"So, Professor?

"Well, he's one of my best friends."

"Who?"

"Heisenberg's Uncertainty Principle, of course. I call him Heis for short."

"A theory is a person?"

"Person, character, sentient being." Ether shrugged. "He's on the Origins Committee too. In fact, he was one of the first things in the Connectome that I helped trace back to your world," the dragon said, puffing out his chest a little. "I'll introduce you to him later."

"What about a musical composition? How does it manifest here?"

"Well, there's one that's like this series of notes floating through the air. You can see it and hear it. It's called Beets-in-the-oven, and we think it's by someone named F. Symphony."

Ian thought about this for several seconds.

"Does it sound like this, by any chance?" He hummed a few bars, beginning with the iconic *da da da duuuum*.

"Yes!" Ether clapped, delighted. "That's it!"

"Right," Ian said. "That would be the Fifth Symphony by Beethoven."

"Oh," Ether said, looking confused. He produced his notepad. "Well, that changes a few things."

"I'm sure it does," Ian said dryly.

Ether looked at him and grinned again. "See? You've been helpful already."

Ian stifled a yawn. "Good. I'll be even more help after a good night's sleep. Freefall takes a lot out of you. And that fire is so cozy . . ."

"I know exactly what you mean. You can have the bed. I'll sleep outside."

"You sure?"

"Positive. Dragon-shaped beds are hard to come by outside of our normal living areas, so we're used to snoozing in all sorts of places. And it will get too warm in here otherwise." Ether shuffled out the door.

Ian stripped down to his underwear and grabbed the blanket off the floor. It was scratchy, but not unbearably so, and the tunic folded up into a serviceable pillow. When he was comfortable, he called out, "Night, Ether."

"Night, Ian."

"Goodnight, John-Boy," something in the darkness added.

Ian jumped out of bed and looked around. Nothing moved. He searched under the bed, beneath the covers, and behind the shelves. Nothing. Still nervous, he climbed back into the bed. It was a long time before he fell asleep.

\* \* \*

IAN AWOKE to the sound of Ether's voice. He sat up, blinking. Ether was warming up another kettle of water. He seemed to be alone.

"Who were you talking to?" Ian asked.

"The fire," Ether replied. "It's very friendly."

"Good morning," it crackled happily.

Ian shook his head. "That's more than I can take first thing in the morning," he said. "I had hoped the weirder stuff from yesterday was a dream."

"You really have to get a better grip on reality." Ether

handed him the last of the jerky and a mug of tea. "Here. This should make things better."

Ian looked closely at Ether. His eyes seemed a little red and puffy. "You don't look so good. What's wrong?"

"Nothing." Ether sniffed. "Just allergies. The trees are pollinating."

"Is there anything you can take?" Ian tried hard not to think about the implications of a dragon with allergies. "A potion or something?"

"Pfft. Potions indeed! This is the Connectome, not Earth's Middle Ages, Ian. I've got some antihistamine at my apartment. We can go grab some if it gets bad."

"You . . . live in an apartment?"

"Of course I do." Ether gave him an indignant look. "Where did you think I lived? Out on the street?"

"Er, no. I guess I was thinking cave or something. On a pile of gold?"

"No." Ether sighed, a dreamy expression creeping into his eyes. "But there is one mountain pad I would love to move into."

Ian smirked. "Let me guess. Ginger's place."

"Maaaaybe."

"Why, Ether, I think you're blushing! You must have it pretty bad."

Ether nodded sadly. "I do. She's absolutely gorgeous."

"Have you talked to her? Asked her out?"

"Are you kidding? She wouldn't give a dragon like me the time of day." Ether stood up and abruptly changed the subject. "Are you just about ready? We should get going."

Ian slurped his tea and hurriedly chewed the jerky. If anything, it tasted even better than it had last night. They tidied up and carefully put out the fire. Before long, they were strolling through the trees again.

It was another beautiful day. Away from the fire and in

the shade of the trees, it seemed a bit cool, but Ian could tell it was going to warm up fairly quickly. He scratched his chin ruefully.

"Wish I'd thought to bring a shaving kit with me," he said. "This is going to itch like crazy until it grows in properly."

"Wasn't there a sword or knife in the cabin?"

"A dagger," he said, patting the scabbard.

"Shave with that, then."

"A straight blade with no soap or water? No thanks."

"Wimp."

"Wimp? Do you have any idea what that would do to my skin?"

The dragon shrugged. "But Drexel the Rugged does it all the time. He's one of this district's top questing champions."

"And what does Drexel look like?"

"Fine, I guess . . . if you're into scars."

"My point exactly. I'll stick with an itchy chin."

"Suit yourself. But in the meantime, hop on."

"I beg your pardon?"

"Get on my back. I'm taking you to see the Flux first. We'll fly there and then walk back." Ether winked at him. "Besides, you knew this had to happen. At some point, every human travelling with a dragon has to go aloft. You get to hang on for dear life while I get to do all kinds of nauseating aerial stunts."

Ian laughed. Now that Ether mentioned it, it did seem appropriate somehow. This was turning out to be fun. "It would be better if I were a grumbly old dwarf who'd spent his life underground."

Ether moved through the trees until he found a clearing, and then he crouched and spread his wings. "You've already got the grumbly part down to a science. You'll have to remember to scream in all the right places. Now, are you going to get on, or do I have to call you a wimp again?"

Ian took a running jump and landed heavily. "Ho, mighty steed!" he shouted and pointed skyward.

"Ooof!" Ether grunted. "Just for that, I've added *two* barrel rolls to the flight plan."

The muscles of Ether's back legs bunched, and his wings tensed. He pushed off with a mighty leap, his claws digging deep into the earth and tossing up great clods of earth. His wings slammed downward, and the leaves on the surrounding trees flinched away from the rush of air. A couple of spine-jarring jerks later, they were fully airborne. Ian wrapped his arms around Ether's neck and hung on for dear life. Dragon scales were way more slippery than they looked.

Ian looked down at the ground. The forest spread out beneath them in a vast green oval. To the east, where the tree line ended, a series of green hills began and then became progressively larger and more rolling as they disappeared into the distance. Ian had flown in a plane before, but this . . . so close and yet so far from the ground . . . in the open air . . . he couldn't help it—he let out a long, heartfelt whoop of enthusiasm.

Ether chuckled, the sound vibrating through his body. "That's where I live," he said, noting the direction of Ian's gaze. "Valleyview Terrace Apartments. The mountains are beyond that."

To the west was a large expanse of flat prairie land, covered in sweet young grass and new spring wildflowers. Peering out over the horizon, Ian thought he could make out a settlement.

Ether banked left. "Any requests? Loops? Spirals? We might as well make it a fun trip."

Ian thought for a moment. "Where does that mouse live? You know . . . that bookie wannabe who was doing a bit of schadenfreude profiteering when I fell through."

"Honest Ed? Just down there." Ether pointed. "Why?"

* * *

"TWENTY-TWO, TWENTY-THREE, TWENTY-FOUR, TWENTY-FIVE," said the mouse, piling up the walnuts. He scratched the number on a leaf. "Not bad for a couple of days' work."

He checked the pile again, frowning when he saw a black mark on the top nut. He licked his paw and attempted to wipe it off. Instead of coming off, the mark slowly got bigger.

It was then that he noticed the sound. It was faint, but it sounded like screaming. One, maybe two people . . . screaming way off in the distance somewhere.

He stood up on his hind legs, looking in all directions, whiskers flicking. He couldn't see anyone nearby, and on this part of the broad, flat meadow, he could see for quite a distance.

Meanwhile, the black mark got bigger. Pretty soon, it covered the entire nut pile and spread toward Ed. Its shape changed rapidly, going from an indistinct blot to a circle with sticks poking out either side.

Ed scuttled up onto a rock to get a better look. It almost looked like a body with a set of wings.

He stopped moving. A horrible thought formed in his head and vibrated down his suddenly rigid body. The hair on the back of his neck rose, and his nose wriggled uncontrollably.

He looked up. "Oh, help!" he said.

He ran for it.

The shadow grew larger, and the screaming grew louder.

"Pull up!" screamed one voice.

"I can't!" screamed the other.

"AAAaaaaagggggghhhh!" they screamed together.

Ed ran as fast as his little legs could carry him, but the

shadow grew faster and outpaced him. He spun around and threw up his little arms in a futile attempt to brace for impact.

Ether pulled up at the last possible second, his tail brushing the top of the nut pile. The wake of his passing caught Ed full force, knocking him backward through a pile of leaves—*whoosh*—over a stack of fallen branches—*bipeta bipeta bipeta*—down a stream bank and into the water.

*Splish!*

A few seconds later, Ed surfaced, spewing water from between his two front teeth. He shook a tiny fist at the retreating dragon and rider.

"I'm going to kill them!" he said.

* * *

THEY FLEW for another half an hour, the warm sunshine doing very little at their altitude to keep Ian from shivering. He was about to ask Ether to fly lower when he spotted a strange sight dead ahead. It was an immense column of bright purple light stretching from the ground all the way up to the sky before disappearing into the clouds.

"What the heck is that?" Ian shouted over the wind.

"That," Ether said, redoubling his speed, "is the Flux."

Ian gripped the dragon tighter, watching in awe as they flew closer. What had seemed at a distance to be a straight beam had now resolved into a roiling, pulsing tornado of crackling purple energy. The air around them thrummed as though they were near an electric transformer, and Ian could sense the hair on the back of his neck prickling. It had to be at least as big around the base as the entire town of Teisburg.

Ether abruptly nosed downward. "We'll land here," he called back over his shoulder. "We can't get too close or we'll go deaf from the noise."

The dragon stretched out and stiffened his wings, setting them on a gentle, gradual glide path to the ground. After several minutes, he touched down gracefully. Ian slid off, shook his arms and legs to ward off cramping, and craned his neck to look up. The Flux seemed to extend upward forever.

Ian pointed at dark shapes that seemed to be caught up in the Flux, some spiralling slowly down the column and others seemingly doing slow circuits along the circumference of the funnel. "What are those?"

"Those are the things from your world in their embryonic form. The stuff starts at the top and, as it becomes more substantive, moves down. Eventually, it's released at the bottom." Ether patted his torso as though looking for something. After a few moments of rummaging under various scales, he pulled out a pair of binoculars and handed them to Ian.

Raising them to his eyes, Ian focused on the base of the column. "I see . . . cats? Hundreds . . . no, *thousands* of cats."

Ether groaned. "Still? It's been doing that for ages. Makes it hard to see what else is coming through the Flux."

"Awwww. They're so cute."

"Ugh," Ether muttered. "What *is* it with you guys and cats? I'd have thought you would have gotten over this back in ancient Egyptian times. Cats don't even like humans that much! Now dogs I could just about understand."

"Oh gosh, Ether. You have to see what this one is doing."

"Ack! Stop already." Ether snatched the binoculars back. "You're just helping to make more."

Ian massaged the back of his neck. The constant hum of the Flux was already starting to give him a headache. "So, wait . . . You said it's been doing cats for a while. Does that mean the link between worlds is in real time?"

"Sort of, yes. In general, it seems to be that whatever a

certain number of humans is attending to or thinking about comes through here at roughly the same time, hence all the stupid cats," Ether waved irritably at the Flux. "But because you guys are also constantly losing information, creating it, and rediscovering it, some things fade, some things are strengthened, and some things come through multiple times. That does some seriously weird stuff with the space–time relationship. Things don't always come through the same way they were created either, like I said. And that interwebs of yours really seems to muck up the timeline and send through crazy stuff. Don't even get me started on the dude with the pompadour singing that annoyingly catchy pop song. I really wish he *would* give me up."

"You mean the Internet," Ian said, shading his eyes to try to see the top of the Flux. "Where does it all go? Stuff from the Flux, I mean. How far back in time did this start happening? How big is the Connectome?"

"Whoa, whoa! That's a lot of questions all at once!" Ether chuckled. "Best way to think of it is like one of your cosmological theories. The Connectome starts here and expands outward in all directions."

Suddenly, Ian was excited. "Really? Does that mean all the oldest stuff is at the edges? Can we go see it?" Being able to see the beginnings of human consciousness and thought was bound to be inspirational. It also sounded incredibly cool.

"Again, sort of. Roughly speaking, it's the oldest stuff at the outskirts and newer stuff at the centre, but we move around a bit . . . group together. Dragons like to hang out with other dragons . . . that sort of thing. But yeah, I suppose we could go all the way out. Hmm." Ether tapped his chin. "Flying would take for-*ever*, but I wonder . . ." He suddenly sprang into the air. Ian watched him fly a few hundred metres up and twist around, looking for something. "Aha!

You're in luck!" he shouted and swooped down again. "There's a ley line over there. Come on."

"A ley what?"

"Ley line. Think of it as an express route."

They walked east for a few minutes until they came upon a long purple scar on the landscape; it was about as wide as a sidewalk, extending straight out from the Flux and disappearing into the distance. Here, the sound of the energy was so loud that it caused the ground underneath Ian's feet to vibrate. The air smelled of ozone.

Ether extended a claw. "Grab on. We'll ride this out to the edge. Step on and off when I do, but not before, or it will take me ages to find you again."

Ian grabbed Ether's talon, and they stepped on the ley line together. Everything smeared into whiteness.

\* \* \*

A SPLIT second and an eternity later, Ether tugged him off the line. Ian stopped screaming, grabbed his head, staggered around wildly, walked straight into a tree, fell over, and threw up.

"Ew," said the dragon.

"What. The Hell," Ian panted, "Was That?"

"A waste of a good breakfast, apparently."

Ian collapsed and rolled onto his back, throwing an arm over his eyes. "Ether," he growled.

"The ley line. I told you. Express travel. There's sixteen of them now, I think. A new set of four—one for each quadrant of the Connectome—appears when the Connectome expands. They're awesome, aren't they?"

"They're *awful*," Ian groaned. "You could have warned me. That was like the worst part of any fairground ride I have ever had the misfortune to be on."

"What's wrong with you?"

"Nothing, except that my head and my stomach are still back where we started."

"Uh, there's some evidence over here that suggests otherwise."

Ian sat up gingerly. "Figure of speech, dragon. Motion sickness. You mean to tell me that didn't bother you? I felt like I was in a centrifuge. A really flipping fast centrifuge. That was also going in a straight line. I can't really describe it, except that it was even worse than falling out of the sky."

"Huh." Ether came over and prodded him. "You really are delicate things, aren't you?"

"Do that again and you better stand back." Ian shifted, suddenly uncomfortable. "Ow! What the heck?" He reached under his legs and pulled out a rock. Still uncomfortable, he shifted again and pulled out two more rocks. It was then that he saw that the ground was littered with them. He frowned and took a closer look at the one he had in his hand. It was shaped like an axe head. "Say, Ether, these aren't stone tools, are they?"

"Took you long enough to notice."

Ian stood up and looked around. There were hammers and hand axes everywhere. "There must be *hundreds* of these things!"

"Humanity has a very, very long history of littering."

The landscape was sand-coloured, dotted with scrub and the occasional short tree. They looked to be in the middle of a gorge, its tall, rocky walls rising on either side of them. Amongst the stone tools, there were animal bones.

"This looks like the pictures I've seen of . . . Africa." Ian was suddenly embarrassed to realize he didn't know *which* country in Africa he was thinking of, Africa being a continent and all. "Why all the tools though?"

Ether beckoned him forward, and they started walking to

the edge of the gorge. "Tools were one of your first ideas, and the process of how to make them was one of the first things you shared."

The farther from the middle of the gorge they got, the more sophisticated the tools became. By the time they reached the gorge wall, the ground was littered with fierce-looking spear and arrow points, carefully knapped into lethal sharpness. Ether flew to the top of the gorge, leaving Ian to scrabble up a steep path. Ether was sunning himself when Ian finally peeked over the top. He was about to say something sarcastic to the dragon about not needing a workout now, when a movement on the horizon made him glance in that direction. His breath caught in his throat.

"What are *those*?"

Enormous humanoid creatures, bigger than any skyscraper Ian had ever seen, half walked, half floated over the ground. They had huge bulbous heads with no distinct features other than overlarge black eyes and a hint of a nose. They reached down now and then, pointing at the ground, and where they did, plants, animals, and humans sprang into life.

"We think they're called Wandjina. From one of the Aboriginal cultures of Australia. Over there," Ether pointed to a fantastically tall woman making mountains and islands and carrying the mud for her work in her hanbok, "is Mago-halmi of modern-day Korea. And there," he pointed in a different direction, to a beautiful copper-skinned woman descending from the sky on the back of a giant turtle, "is Sky Woman. From indigenous cultures in your part of the world, I believe."

Ian finished his climb and slowly turned around. On the other side of the gorge were giant eggs—some golden, some transparent, and some in the process of cracking in half. A few looked to contain stars, moons, and planets, while others looked like they had sky and earth enclosed. In another area, a giant god first vomited up a group of animals that included a white heron and a crocodile and then moved on to heave up some humans. Ian winced and rubbed his stomach. "These are . . . these are creation stories, aren't they?" he said.

"Yes. As you can see, there's quite a variety." Ether stretched and jerked a thumb to indicate a path leading away from the gorge's edge. "You're probably thirsty with all that climbing. There's a nice tavern up the way. They do a really good pale ale there. It comes in pints."

Ian wasn't sure he wanted a beer this early in the day, but on the other hand, the bubbles might help settle his stomach. "A tavern? That doesn't seem truly . . . prehistoric."

Ether started strolling away. "Like I said, the timelines aren't geographically exact because we have free will here and move around. But you all've been making beer since forever, so it kind of works."

Ian jogged to catch up, trying not to be too goggle-eyed as they passed by a seated deity making a human figure out of maize. The path twisted, turned, and started angling slightly downhill, eventually leading them to the biggest tavern Ian had ever seen. The sign said "GOD'S HEAD." They went inside.

The interior seemed many times larger than even the exterior would have indicated, and it was packed. The air inside was cool and smelled strongly of yeast and hops. There was lively music being played somewhere. At a table near the entrance, a blue-skinned god with four arms was playing cards against four opponents: an elephant, a man with a falcon head, a feathered serpent that looked distinctly unhappy with the hand it had been dealt, and an older white male in long flowing robes who had a magnificent beard. Ian stared, fascinated, until Ether tugged on his sleeve.

"C'mon," said the dragon. "There's usually a nice spot up at the bar. Whatever you do, don't make eye contact with—"

Just then, a well-muscled man in a toga sidled up to Ian. "Heeeey, handsome," he said.

"—Zeus." Ether sighed. "Keep walking," he mouthed at Ian.

"Hi?" Ian said, nodding politely as he brushed past the man to trail Ether.

Zeus was undeterred. He followed them, sat on a stool beside Ian, and leaned back against the bar with both elbows. The top of his toga flopped open strategically to reveal a godly bare chest and a garish gold chain necklace with a lightning bolt pendant. "You're awfully cute. Has anyone ever told you that?"

"Not lately, no. But thank you." The strong tang of body spray wafted over and made Ian's eyes sting.

"So, listen . . . trying to show my boy here the ways of the world, if you get my meaning," Zeus said, waggling his eyebrows and jerking a thumb back toward a much younger man in the crowd. He wore a sullen expression and stood with his shoulders hunched and arms crossed against his chest. He spotted Zeus looking at him and glowered back. Zeus turned back to Ian and rolled his eyes. "He's sooo hung up on this Phoebe character, but I want him to live a little before settling down. Whaddya say?"

Ian accepted a beer from Ether. "I'm sorry . . . what do I say to what?"

"Me and the dragon, you and the boy. You know, a little Pollux and chill?" Zeus gave him an exaggerated wink.

Ian sputtered into his drink. "Oh, ah, see, I'm flattered . . ."

"Don't be," Ether mumbled into his own mug.

" . . . but no thanks. I'm, ah, not looking for anything right now."

"Really? That's too bad. I mean, I suppose you're no Ganymede, but it could have been fun."

Ian nearly choked again and resolved not to take another sip for a while. "Did you . . . did you just try to neg me?"

Zeus had the grace to look slightly embarrassed. "What if I offered to smite you? You into that? What about swans?"

"No!"

The deity slumped a little. "Hey, I had to try." Zeus spotted a woman in the crowd and brightened immediately. "Mnemosyne, baby!" he called, smoothing back the hair at his temples and fluffing his beard. "Remember me?" He dashed off in pursuit. Pollux, seeing what Zeus was doing, huffed away in the opposite direction.

"Sorry about that. I didn't think he'd be so quick," Ether said. "He must monitor the door for new blood."

They sat in companionable silence for a while, sipping and god-watching. The beer on an empty stomach was quickly giving Ian a nice buzz and loose limbs, which seemed rather decadent at this time of day. And as weird as everything was in the Connectome, he found he was more relaxed than he had been in months. Indeed, as his shoulders unknotted and eased back down, he realized that he didn't know how tense and stressed he'd been. Perhaps, he mused, that's what was giving him writer's block. As he surveyed the crowd of gods, demi-gods, random heroes, and animistic spirits, he decided that he was going to absorb the experiences, take it all in, and let his subconscious do some background processing rather than trying to pull story ideas out just yet. "So where to after this?" he asked. "Or should I say when to?"

"Well, the next super big thing after tool making is agriculture."

"Ugh . . . farming," Ian muttered.

Beside him, a tall creature he hadn't noticed before now

whipped around to fix him with a hard stare. It was a gorgeous white fox, standing on its hind legs, its body decorated with stylized red swirls and stripes.

"What, exactly, is wrong with agriculture?"

"Oh, hi, Inari." Ether smiled.

"Ah . . ." Ian swallowed his beer. "It's boring? To me, anyway."

"You eat, right?"

Ian chuckled. "Yes, of course I do. And I know agriculture is important because we have to eat. Believe me, I live around farmers. They have tons of bumper stickers about this sort of thing. It's still not a topic I care much about."

"I have no idea what a 'bumper sticker' is, but fine." Inari nodded. "Did you also know that agriculture is responsible for civilization as you know it? It's one of the most important things humans ever came up with, right up there with the ability to control fire."

"Well, yeah, I guess. Basic history. People were able to settle down, store food, specialize in different kinds of jobs . . . that sort of thing." Ian took a big swig of his brew, and an impish urge overtook him. "You know, though, that there is an argument that agriculture was the worst thing that ever happened to humanity."

"Ian," Ether hissed. He tried to covertly make a shushing gesture.

"According to this theory, it brought about famines, disease, social inequalities . . ."

Ether tried waving and making stopping motions, drawing a talon across his throat.

" . . . wars, and so on. There's also the idea that modern, intensive agriculture has been horrendous for the environment."

Ether stuck his head directly between Inari and Ian. "Did I mention Inari is a *kami*?"

Inari gently pushed Ether aside and regarded Ian archly. Ian had just a few moments to wonder what powers a kami might have and to contemplate whether he was about to be smote after all.

"What did humans get from agriculture?" she said.

"Like I said, settling down, different kinds of jobs . . ."

"They got to settle by good water sources."

"Sure, but—"

"They were able to do more elaborate crafting and tool-making because they could stay put."

"Okay, and—"

"They were able to store food and support larger populations, which ensured the survival of the species. They could defend themselves better. Child mortality trended down over time. Life expectancy went up over time. They had much richer and more varied social structures. They started writing. They started organized religion. They began investigating the world around them using rudimentary science. They started creating more literature. More art. They began creating *philosophy*. Are those things worthless?"

"No, but—"

Ether began gently bonking his head on the bar.

"And there is the argument that hunting was the cause of a lot of extinctions, resulting in a lack of food, and that depending more on farming might have been the way out of that crisis."

"Um—"

"So, essentially, humans traded one type of crisis for a somewhat better type of crisis. Like they did with the whole industrial thing. And cars and horses later."

"Er—"

Inari threw back her drink and whacked the glass down on the bar surface. "Human history is basically a series of cost–benefit calculations. But they rarely take all the costs into account and then work to make those ratios better for everyone. So the problem is not agriculture. The problem is that humans need to get much better at *math*." She sniffed haughtily. "I don't know what you're the demi-god of, but it's sure not *smarts*." She spun on her heels, her big white fluffy tail whacking Ian upside the head, and marched off.

The tavern seemed to spin suddenly, and everything around him grew exponentially larger. Ian felt like he was in freefall again, and suddenly, he was on the floor looking up. He heard Ether scramble off his seat and then saw the dragon extend a ginormous talon that picked him up between thumb and forefinger before carefully setting him on the barstool. Ether waited.

After several minutes, there was a rushing sound in Ian's ears, and everything was back to normal.

Ether clapped slowly. "Well done, Ian. You were completely outclassed and outfoxed."

"What the heck happened?" Ian grumbled, rubbing the side of his head. "Why was she so keen on farming anyway?"

"She turned you into a grain of rice. You picked a fight with a *kami* of agriculture about agriculture. That's two gods you've annoyed in less than fifteen minutes. I'd hate to see what kind of trouble you'd get into on *two* beers. Maybe not interact with any more deities for a bit?"

"Your fault. My stomach is empty."

Ether grinned and waved at the bartender. "Food! Why didn't you remind me of that earlier? Time for something to eat."

* * *

THEY POLISHED off a meal that could have been brunch or lunch or both and made their way to the back door of the tavern. Ian shoved open the exit with great difficulty and stepped out to find himself surrounded on all sides by piles and piles of . . .

"What on earth is all of this?" he asked, bewildered.

"Potsherds," Ether said, reaching for a handful.

"There must be thousands of the things!"

Ether nodded. "Like I said, humans have a long history of littering."

Ian looked at the piles of broken pottery. "Ordinarily, I'd say you were being too judgmental, but yikes. Have we really left this many behind?"

"You sure have. I've never understood why humans continue to make their food and drink containers out of something so *fragile*. And you haven't learned in thousands of years."

Ian put his hands on his hips. "Hey, we don't use amphorae for wine anymore."

Ether gave him a look. "And what do you use?"

"Okay, glass, but . . ."

"And those dishes in your kitchen? Are they tin?"

"Ceramics," Ian said weakly, thinking about the coffee cup he had dropped only a few weeks ago. "What is this? Gang-up-on-Ian day?"

Ether patted him kindly. "Fair enough. But yes, you've left lots of these behind. I'm glad I wasn't near the Flux when these came pelting through. It must have been a real sherd-storm." The dragon handed him some cotton balls. "Here. You'll need these soon."

"What for?" Ian asked as they began wending their way through the mountains of broken pottery. "Do I want to know?"

"Nothing too scary," the dragon replied. "We've seen the stone tools, the creation stories, the beginnings of religion and spirituality, and you know about agriculture. I'm assuming you know what fire looks like and don't need to travel through the Valley of Flames in person?"

"Uh, yeah. I get that fire was an important thing. I really don't need to be barbecued today as well as everything else."

"Good, good. The next big section of the Connectome is all about the first time humans began outsourcing their mental functions."

"What?"

"Artificial memory storage systems."

"Still not following."

Ether paused and stuffed the cotton in his ears. "Tools were extensions of your physical abilities. Now, think language, Ian. Especially written language. You found a way to extend and even transmit your memories by writing things down. And boy howdy did you come up with a lot of languages."

Ian stuffed his own cotton balls into his ears as they cleared the shard piles. The land ahead was barren desert with nothing but a long, narrow pathway through sand dunes stretching out in front of them. At first, all was silent. As they walked along the path, Ian became aware of words being repeated over and over again. He strained to listen to them. It sounded like "ciao mondu." They walked farther, and another chorus joined in, this time saying "përshendetje botë." And another, and another, and another until all Ian could hear was a cacophony of phrases.

. . . Բարեւ աշխարհ salam dünyası moni dziko lapansi 你好世界 kumusta sa mundo hei maailma salve mundi ndewo uwa 안녕 세상 qo' vIvan Привет мир dia duit ar domhan hallo welt ਸਤਿ ਸ੍ਰੀ ਅਕਾਲ ਦੁਨਿਆ alofa fiafia i le lalolagi . . .

Ian clapped his hands over his ears and began jogging as the noise became unbearable. As they progressed through the desert, the dune morphed into giant stone tablets, and then massive papyrus scrolls, and finally into gargantuan leather-bound books fastened to the ground by enormous chains.

"This is wild!" Ian shouted at Ether.

Ether handed him more cotton and leaned close so Ian could hear. "The next bit is even louder. It's where we cut through the Time Plains, where all of your attempts to track time have congregated. It'll get easier after that, though!"

Ian didn't have a chance to ask for more details before Ether trotted off. Ian matched his brisk pace, and as the voices faded away, the ground gradually changed from shifting sand to dirt and the area around them became a grassy expanse. Ian looked down in time to see something slithering through the grass. "Agh! Snake!" he shouted and leaped backward.

Ether laughed. "Look closer."

Dubious, Ian cautiously followed the movement through the grass until he caught sight of what he was chasing. "It's a knotted rope!"

"Quipu," Ether nodded. "Now, look up."

Ian glanced at the sky and whooped with delight. Approaching from the west was a huge flock of what could only be calendars, flapping and honking and bleating like geese. "That's ridiculous!"

They paused to watch them fly directly overhead. Ether pulled out his binoculars and a notebook. "Ooh! These are Babylonian. You can tell by the crescent moon markings." He made a checkmark on a list in the book.

"This doesn't seem too bad noise-wise?"

"Wait until we get to the watering hole."

They followed the calendars, and sure enough, the noise level rose as they approached the gathering place. They ducked down behind a small knoll, and Ether handed him the binoculars. Ian was certainly no expert, but even he could guess at the different types based on the symbols and lettering: lunar, solar, Hebrew, Islamic, Hindu and Chinese, and dozens more, all chirping and tweeting and flapping and splashing. A squabble broke out on the other side of the pond, and there was a flurry of loose pages.

"Salvador Dali has nothing on this place," Ian murmured.

"Come on!" Ether clapped him on the back. "Horologia Proper is this way."

Ether led him Fluxward, and the sound of flapping calendars was soon replaced with the sound of ticking. Ian had a feeling he knew what was coming.

The path they'd been following vanished, and the ticking grew louder. They picked their way through a field of sundials glinting in the bright light, and the ticking was now accompanied by tocking noises, and water dripping, and the whooshing noise of immense quantities of sand falling through narrow glass tubes.

Ian stopped and covered his ears again. They were now surrounded by clocks, watches, hourglasses, and clepsydras, some of them tiny, some of them monumental. The scene was a dizzying array of gears and swinging pendulums, clanking, creaking chains and motorized figurines, and blinking, flashing LED lights. Ian stared, completely fascinated. It was a precise mechanical ballet and a crazy circus all rolled into one. If it weren't for the noise, it would be incredibly satisfying to sit and watch it all moving around.

Ether, his own ears flattened against his head, suddenly became very pale. He grabbed Ian's shoulder to shake it and pointed at a nearby clock face. It read one minute to noon.

"Oh no," Ian said. "Talk about bad timing. That doesn't mean they're all going to . . ."

"RUN!" Ether shouted, and he loped off.

Ian scrambled after him, running flat out to keep up. He squeezed past the carved wooden frame of an hourglass and had to leap on top of another timepiece to avoid the massive brass pendulum of a nearby grandfather clock. He ran some more, braked, and backed away from a gear, only to have the back of his shirt hooked on a fast-moving second hand from some other clock that swung him up even higher off the ground. He squirmed until he broke free, landing on the roof of a building. Ian spun around and ran full tilt into a clock tower marked *Puerta del Sol*. He staggered, landed flat on his back, and groaned.

All of a sudden, the sky was full of dragon. Ether had grown bigger again, and he swooped low, catching Ian in both talons before straining upward.

And then thousands of clocks hit the hour.

*BONG!*

*CRASH!*

*DING!*

*CLANG!*

*BOOM!*

*BING!*

*CUCKOO!*

Ether was flipped end over end in the turbulence, but he managed to right himself quickly, redoubling his wing stroke until they cleared the edge of the plains. They glided for a while longer until the noise was a distant, painful memory. Finally, they touched down on soft, green grass.

Ian splayed out on the turf. "Sorry about getting so mixed up back there," he said between gasps. "I was trying to keep up, I really was. One minute, I'm on the ground; the next, I'm crashing into the top of a big tower, of all things. I have no idea how that happened."

"That's okay, Ian," Ether panted. "Nobody expects a Spanish imposition."

\* \* \*

ONCE THEY HAD RECOVERED, they resumed their journey.

"I hadn't realized," Ian was saying as they walked, "how much effort we'd devoted to timekeeping. I mean, everything runs to a clock these days, but I guess I have this impression of people in the past being less concerned about it somehow."

"Seasons are important to farming," Ether said, acknowledging Ian's answering grimace at this with a smile. "But also festivals and other social events. Religions are big on calendars. Explorers and mapmakers needed good timepieces too, for making accurate measurements of distance."

"Hey. I just realized we didn't see any star charts in all of that chaos. Weren't those kind of a big deal?"

Ether nodded in agreement. "For sure. It was actually kind of shocking how many stars you can't see where you live, Ian, given how important they were. The charts and theories are generally all grouped near where the creation stories are because they're closely linked. Of course, explorers made use of those too." He pointed east. "Now, over there is a region called Necessary Evils."

"That sounds decidedly ominous."

"Legal codes, taxes, major documents, and ledgers. I'm going to go ahead and assume you don't want to visit."

"Gah, no. Considering how the Time Plains ended up, I could do without being flattened by a monolithic Magna Carta or something."

"Don't be silly," Ether admonished him. "You'd die of boredom first. Don't get me wrong," the dragon stopped to scratch his back against a large tree trunk, "that sort of thing is the basis of human civilization. Without all sorts of rules and regulations to keep chaos at bay, you wouldn't have time to create all the cool things that you do. But there's a reason why I'm not on the Minutiae Subcommittee." He pointed ahead. "Now, this area coming up, this is one of my favourites. I've spent a lot of time here."

They crested a small hill, and beyond it, the land dipped away into a lush green river channel. It was swarming with all manner of beasts and boats, thundering armies, and intrepid adventurers in glorious clothes.

"Whoa," Ian said, looking out over the spectacle.

Ether seemed pleased. "This is the Valley of the Epics. Come sit and watch for a bit."

They found a shady spot on the other side of the hill and sat down.

"This is like a callback to my undergrad," Ian said, his eyes sparkling as he scanned the valley. "This is incredible! I hardly know where to watch first."

Directly below their feet, a Danish hero was busy trying to rip the arm off a scary monster while the men around them cowered in fear. Nearby, a king and a wildman wrestled in a test of strength. Across the river, several men were skulking near a flock of sheep, preparing to escape the clutches of a cyclops.

"So, come on. Show me what you've got," Ether said, leaning back against a tree and crossing his hind legs out in front of him.

"Challenge accepted." Ian pointed to a large wooden horse outside a city gate. "The *Aeneid*, probably. Over there." He indicated a vast battlefield where two Indian forces bristling with bows, maces, swords, lances, and darts were preparing to do battle. "Wow, that's got to be the *Mahabharata*. I've never seen it re-enacted."

"It's truly epic, as it goes on for days and days. I've only managed the first half so far."

"And that," Ian pointed way off into the distance, where he could just make out a woman shouting and cursing at the gates of a city, causing it to burst into flames, "must be Kannagi. I can't remember the name of the poem though."

"*Silappadikaram.*"

"Yes! That's it. Oh my gosh!" Ian jumped up. "That gorgeous Persian court over there. It's magnificent." Ian observed some well-dressed courtiers playing chess, while others listened to a musician. "That must be from *Shahnameh*."

"Ian?"

"What?" Ian said, not taking his eyes off the valley below.

"Your nerd is showing."

Ian laughed and sat back a little. "Sorry. It's one thing to study the texts, it's another to see them brought to life like this."

"Don't be sorry!" Ether reached over and rubbed Ian's shoulder. "Never apologize for being knowledgeable. I was just teasing because you're so into this."

Ian leaned forward again, his eyes darting from one story to another. Ether was right; he *was* into it. With everything that was associated with graduating, getting a job, doing the daily grind at work, and paying the bills, he'd forgotten why he'd gone to school in the first place. Here, seeing the grand history of the epics with all of their pageantry concentrated in one place, he was reminded of how rich the literary traditions of the world were. "And this is just the ancient stuff," he murmured, watching the Finnish blacksmith Ilmarinen forge a magical artifact.

"What?"

"I was thinking that this doesn't even begin to cover the breadth and depth of the stories handed down through time."

"True." Ether stroked his chin. "This stuff has been in the Connectome for a good long time, and it's so vibrant precisely because it's been read and re-imagined by so many of your kind. And it *is* amazing. We've studied these and some of the other stuff I've shown you fairly extensively because they've been here so long. But, to my mind, it's not quite your greatest invention, based on its impact and potential."

Ian glanced back at the dragon. "What's our greatest invention? You mean like the wheel or something?"

"No. The novel."

This had Ian's attention. "Seriously? Like, bigger than transistors and everything? Or even the printing press?"

Ether leaned forward, an intense look on his face. "Think about it. These epics? Usually passed down orally or performed. Consumed in groups. And for the longest time, until spelling and grammar were somewhat standardized, early books had to be read aloud slowly to make them comprehensible. When the novel became a thing—*boom!*" Ether smacked a fist into his other hand. "I've just started reading the early ones. These stories could be intimate. You read them yourself . . . consume them privately. You could take the time to think about them. You could live dozens or hundreds of other lives vicariously and cheaply. You could begin to understand what was going on in someone else's head. You could *empathize.* I'm convinced the novel will go down in your history as when humanity started becoming humane."

"Ether?"

"Yes?"

"Your nerd is showing."

"Darn right!" Ether snorted.

"I dunno though. We've had an awful lot of wars and revolutions and other horrible things at the same time as we've had novels."

Ether stood up on all fours and stretched, one appendage at a time. "With an increasing number of people saying it maybe wasn't such a good idea to do that each time. You're still very much a work in progress."

"Ain't that the truth."

"Speaking of progress, come on. It's time to really blow your mind."

\* \* \*

ETHER FLEW them across the valley and beyond, allowing Ian a glimpse of what he was sure amounted to Dante's *Inferno* below. They then travelled through a brief and terrifying void.

"The concept of zero, Ian!" Ether cheerfully explained. "Very important, especially in mathematics!"

Fortunately, they were out of the void before Ian's existential dread became overwhelming. From there, they flew low into the giant stone works of Megalithia, slipping between dolmen and menhirs, circling the henges, brushing by moai and stelae, and some colossal Olmec heads. Eventually, they found themselves on the outskirts of a large city.

The buildings that towered above them were of all shapes and sizes and surrounded by trees, and some of them were covered with vines and topped with thatched roofs. There were no vehicles; the residents, all garbed in traditional clothing from a variety of African countries, bustled past storefronts or stopped to buy woven baskets, with some lingering by street carts brimming with tempting hot food. Ether stopped to buy something tasty on a skewer.

"This whole area," Ether slurped, "is the Technocity. Mostly your visions of the future, but it's also where a lot of the science and engineering concepts hang out, because, well, nerds of a feather flock together. This side is the utopian portion. The other side is all dark nights, pouring rain, stinky markets selling illegal things, neon lights, and too many dreary, oppressive, brutalist buildings."

Glancing around him, Ian was glad they'd arrived on this side of the city. They walked farther into the centre, and the buildings changed to tall, sleek affairs—all glass and steel and sunlight. Flying cars buzzed so low that they made Ian flinch. There were robots everywhere—some blocky and bristling with old-school transistor tubes and antennae and others smooth, shiny, and polished to perfection. Ian saw cyborgs too—some with little more than a funky set of glasses and others that were nearly half machine. Somewhere nearby, they could hear the rumble of a rocket taking off.

"Oh yes! Since we're here, you should see this too," Ether said as they approached an overlarge beehive with two entrances; it looked incongruously organic in the middle of all of this technology. "The financial district! You'll find this interesting. That," he gestured at the hive, "is, of course, one of your essential monetary innovations: double-entry beekeeping."

"Wait, what? No . . . hang on—"

But Ether had already disappeared behind the structure. Ian hurried after him and then skidded to a stop. Money—everything from bills to beads to strange round coins with square holes in the middle—was literally flowing through the air from one place to another. But that wasn't all. In the capacious open market that spread out before him were piles of all kinds of trade goods, including spices, silk, salt, cattle, self-sealing stem bolts, wine, toys, and food. Traders, dressed in a variety of outfits from the distant past and all the way into an imagined future, talked noisily about an infinite number of transactions.

Ian watched everything change hands over and over again. "That's . . . a lot of filthy lucre."

"Hmm," Ether agreed. "Although it's interesting you should refer to it that way. Ever since I found this place, I've wondered about the weird love–hate relationship you have with this kind of thing. You describe money with adjectives like 'obscene,' yet it's actually one of the more enduring symbols of trust between strangers you've ever come up with. Being able to assign values and agree upon them."

"Depends on who's doing the valuation, I suppose." Ian ducked as a stream of gold coins whizzed past his ear. "As applied to things, it's not too bad. When it's assigned to beings, it becomes a pretty cold calculus. I mean in big lump sums, it can do amazing stuff like fund space exploration or a search for a cure for cancer. I don't think anyone really objects to that sort of thing. I suppose it's when you see how much money some megacorporations make selling things while at the same time offloading costs onto little places like Teisburg that it starts to piss you off."

"Eh? How does that happen?"

"Well, it's like when you raided my kitchen and there were all those containers—"

"Jeez, Ian, I said sorry."

"No, no, listen. I mean, at least the cans were recyclable. But there's so much crap that isn't, and it's not properly compostable either. Like the big coffee chains that make their money selling coffee. All that supposedly disposable stuff—the cups, the lids, the stir sticks, the milk cartons . . . stuff that's cheap to the company—all of that gets dumped in the trash, and it's up to guys like Mayor Harry to find the money to get rid of it. And there's disposable razors and Styrofoam trays and diapers and plastic bags. We've run out of places to hide the stuff." Ian puffed out his cheeks in frustration. "We need way better regulations."

"Ian, I had no idea you were a communionist."

"What? Oh, you mean communist. I'm not, although you'd think I would be." He thought about his short and sad employment history. "No, I'm not really right or left wing. I mean, I don't think something simple like 'don't foul your own nest' should be a partisan debate." He shrugged. "I don't know where I am politically. I keep meaning to check out what the Nordic countries are doing, as everyone says they seem to be getting it right."

"What's a Nord?"

Ian laughed. "No such thing. Nordic means the country . . . like Sweden and Denmark."

"Oh! So you want to be a Viking! Did you know who the chief librarian of the Vikings was?"

"Huh? Uh, no."

"Erik the Read."

Ian face-palmed. "Seriously, Ether?"

"Who raked the Viking's lawns while they were away?"

"I'm sure I don't want to know."

"Leaf Erickson."

"Ether!"

"Sorry. Did that hurt? Perhaps you'd like a hygge to help you feel better?"

"Okay. That one *did* hurt."

"I'll be merciful. One more place to see before we go meet the Origins Committee. Walk this way."

Ian half expected the dragon to do a silly walk, but for once, Ether played it straight. They threaded their way through the financial district and popped out of that region next to an arena called Virtuality Place. Ian, starting to become footsore, looked at it doubtfully. "You're not going to make me play hockey or something, are you? I mean, I may be Canadian and all, but not all of us play it. I don't even know if I could skate properly anymore."

Ether gave him a cheeky grin and walked inside. At the reception booth, a bored-looking youth produced a ticket for Ian.

"You're not coming in?" Ian asked warily.

"Nah. Dragon-sized suits cost extra, and I've been a few times already. I'll wait here."

The teenager cleared his throat noisily; he was holding

the door open. Wondering what he was letting himself in for this time, Ian walked through it.

"First door on your left," the boy said.

They went down a long corridor, and Ian found the door indicated. The room was empty, except for a weird contraption in the centre that looked like a circular moving sidewalk. He went in, and the boy handed him a coverall and a helmet.

"Is this a crash suit?" Ian asked, even more nervous now.

The boy rolled his eyes so hard that Ian thought they were going to fall out. "No. It's a haptic feedback suit. Put it on, and knock on the door to tell me you're ready." The boy left, shaking his head at the stupidity of everyone over the age of twenty.

Ian struggled into the outfit and found gloves and a kind of sock-like thing tucked down one sleeve. He pulled off his shoes, replaced them with the socks—there didn't seem to be any other way to fit them—and pulled on the gloves. He grabbed the helmet, which resembled something you'd wear when riding a motorbike, and pulled it on. He knocked on the door.

Within minutes, everything around him changed. He was in the middle of a big domed room, and in the centre of it, a large telescope stretched upward to the sky. There didn't seem to be anyone around, but looking up through the slot in the ceiling, he could see that it was dark outside. Not knowing what else he should do, he took a step toward the telescope. His surroundings stretched and warped like they were water going down a drain, and he was actively being pulled against his will toward the scope, which loomed larger and larger as he approached. Ian shrank, went spinning into the eyepiece, bounced from mirror to mirror inside the device, and caromed out the end.

Everything went black. His movements, which had

echoed loudly in the big empty room a moment ago, now didn't make a sound. He couldn't even hear himself breathing in the helmet. His suit warmed a little, and then it was as though he wasn't wearing it at all. It reminded him of that one time he'd spent in a float tank; he felt ethereal, discon-nected, and as if he was tumbling gently in an endless absence. It was a little freaky. He took a few deep breaths, reminding himself that it was just a show, but his brain was trying really hard to make him panic.

There, at the edge of his vision, was an infinitesimally small dot. Grateful for a distraction, he tried to focus on it. He blinked, and the dot was gone, replaced by a glorious burst of matter and light racing away from him in all direc-tions. Propelled by some unknown force, he sped away alongside it all, watching as it gathered to form ghostly nebulae that gave birth to bright stars or swirled and coalesced into beautiful spinning galaxies. He floated that way for a while, until the leading edge of the universe gradu-ally outpaced him and spread away beyond the limits of his vision. Ian was dropped into one of the spinning galaxies, like giant celestial Ferris wheels, and it became the familiar milky slash across the night sky that he remembered from his nights in the north as a child.

He veered past a smaller sphere that he recognized from photos as poor demoted Pluto with its heart-shaped plains. Within another eyeblink, he was plunging through the twin-kling icy rings of Saturn, emerging improbably right beside Jupiter over the Great Red Spot, that most ancient of storms. From there, he was flung around Jupiter and sent sailing toward a prehistoric Earth, its continents smushed together into one giant landmass. He plunged into the atmosphere, heat and light licking the sides of the suit, and gasped in amazement as the land below cracked into pieces and began moving across the sea, their shapes getting more and more familiar as Ian kept falling. Where there had been land before, now there was only water; belatedly remembering the swimming and diving lessons from his boyhood, he twisted and pointed his body downward, hands together over his head, entering the water like a missile going the wrong way.

Down, down he sank, hundreds of metres, the water teeming with life around him. Out of the inky depths, a razor-tooth beast six times his size lunged up to bite him, but before its jaws could clamp his legs—before he could even react—the body dissolved, leaving nothing but a skeleton that floated away intact to a ledge of oceanic rock, to be covered in sediment and preserved for eternity. The water boiled all around him, huge bubbles battering him nearly senseless, and a volcano sprang up from the ocean floor under his feet, leaving him scrambling up its half-molten slopes. Ian emerged from the water with a gasp, stumbling across the rapidly expanding island that transformed in an instant to a lush, warm island filled with colourful chattering birds and a colony of noisy seals.

The wind blew hard, tossing him back into the sea. He experienced a moment's profound disorientation. A powerful earthquake wrenched everything around him; he was lifted high up on a tsunami that raced across the ocean and flung him onto land, across a mountain range, and onto a broad, flat, endless prairie. Caught up in another wind, he was spun up from the ground into a writhing tornado; he travelled to the top in a slow, ponderous corkscrew and was spat out again, grabbed by a jet stream, whisked across another ocean, and dumped into a beautiful glen laden with bright purple heather. His landing scared a starling, and then another, and another, and then thousands of them were in the air, turning and wheeling—no longer individual but part of a collective whole. As one, they traced sine waves across the sky, folding and unfolding and turning the pattern inside out, upside down, and back again. It was more glorious than any ballet or any parade ground march that Ian had ever seen. It was at once completely synchronous and entirely effortless.

He turned to see the flock soar overhead, and when he turned again, he was in a lab stuffed full of beakers and magnets and strange-looking devices. Ian was small—he was beginning to wonder how Ether managed not to bump into door frames or stub his toes as his perspective kept changing —and then he was being poked and prodded, superheated over a Bunsen burner, sent sliding down a wire like an electrical current, sucked up by a fume hood, photographed, x-rayed, centrifuged, dropped into agar, stained, smeared onto a glass plate, and slid underneath the lens of a microscope. Now he was floating, rushing along a bloodstream, and battered by red and white cells pinballing around the chambers of the heart. Another blink and he was inside a single cell, crouching, bumping into things he vaguely remembered labelling on an eighth-grade test diagram, getting squeezed now as the cell split into two and the walls vanished completely, and he was climbing up a spiral helix—up . . . up . . . and up until he popped out of a grate in the floor of the observatory once more. Winded and overwhelmed, he staggered and sat down hard as the walls dissolved back into the room in which he'd suited up.

Ether came in to collect him and waited patiently as Ian pulled the helmet off his sweaty head. "That was . . . wild," Ian said, chest heaving from the climb. "The whole scope of it, the macro, the micro . . . I-I . . . sorry. It's going to take me a bit to wrap my head around all of that." He wiped his face. "It gives you a perspective on the wonders of the universe, that's for sure. Mind is definitely blown."

"I don't understand half of what that shows you yet. But,

more than that, Ian," the dragon said, helping him up, "it shows you a tiny fraction of all the things humanity has been able to discover and learn. Not bad for just a few thousand years' work. Think how far your species could go. You should be proud."

Indeed, Ian thought as he peeled out of his suit, he kind of was.

\* \* \*

DONE with their tour for now, they flew for a long time, Ether's great wings pumping at a steady, distance-eating pace. He kept them low to the ground this time so that Ian wouldn't get too cold, skimming just over the young grasses and flowers of the meadows, which seemed to dip and bow as he passed. For a while, with the wind rushing past them, the sun glinting off the dragon scales, and the grace of the flight, Ether seemed almost majestic.

"*Snrk*," Ether snuffled loudly and rubbed his eyes.

Ian laughed. "We should have stopped for your allergy medicine."

"Nah." Ether shook his head. "I'll get something from Heis when we arrive. He's a bit of a hypochondriac, so he usually has something on him. Ah, here we are."

Ether banked gently to the left as a small dwelling came into view. It was a beautiful English-style cottage, its walls painted white and its roof a tidy, thatched masterpiece. The lattice windows sported black flower boxes that overflowed with new blooms. He circled it once, pulled up and extended his back legs, and landed with a minimum of effort. Ian slid off his back and onto the ground.

The door was opened almost immediately by a short, black rabbit. He was holding a brush on a long pole, and he stared goggle-eyed at Ian.

Ether peered at the rabbit. "Good grief, Hutch! What happened? You look like a furry cinder."

Hutch blinked rapidly at Ian and then seemed to focus on what Ether had said. "What? Oh, right. Hang on." He disappeared back into the house for a second and reappeared with a towel in hand. He began rubbing himself vigorously. Clouds of black dust puffed away in the wind. After a great deal of twisting, patting, and squirming, Hutch changed into a light brown rabbit with a cottontail.

"Sorry about that." He smiled. "I was cleaning out the chimney for Heis. That's how I saw you fly in." He turned to Ian. "Is this what I think it is?"

Ether nodded. "Hutch, this is Ian MacDonald. Ian, this is Hutch, Chair of the Origins Committee." Ether paused dramatically. "Ian is from the Other Side, Hutch."

"I can see that! He's completely solid! Not a trace of ethe-reality! How did he get here?"

"I brought him here."

"You brought him? You mean you broke on through to the Other Side? When did this happen? Why didn't you tell anyone you were going? We don't have any safety protocols established! That was incredibly dangerous."

"Erm," Ether said, "well, you know me . . . not much of a fan of bureaucracy. It seemed safe, and I wanted to keep it a surprise." He glared at Ian, daring him to say otherwise. "I didn't want anyone to be disappointed if it didn't work."

"As chair, I have to say we'll discuss the consequences later. Can't have everyone going off on rogue projects. But as a researcher . . ." Hutch scuttled closer to Ian. His whiskers thrummed, and his eyes twinkled with delight. He sat up and extended a paw. "Welcome!"

"Hello," said Ian, thinking that he'd been shaking some awfully strange appendages in the last few days.

"Whoa." Hutch shivered all over at the sound of Ian's

voice. "You sound so different from the humans we've seen through the rifts. No distortion." He started bouncing from one back foot to the other. "I have a thousand questions to ask you. But first, we *must* have you meet the rest of the committee!" He hippity-hopped back to the door and stuck his head inside. "Hey, everyone! Come quick!"

Ian leaned closer to Ether. "He's the *chair* of the committee? How cute!"

Ether winced. "Whatever you do, don't let him hear you say that. He tries very hard to be taken seriously."

"But that cottontail?"

"Yup. But trust me on this. Check out his ear tattoo if you don't believe me."

Hutch came back with three friends in tow. "Ian? This is Mr. Power."

A pale, vaguely humanoid figure stepped forward rather hesitantly. He was thin and scrawny, and he seemed to have trouble focusing. His handshake was rather limp.

"You can c-c-call me Will," he said quietly. He nodded at Ether. "Nice to see you again, Ether."

"And this," Hutch continued, "is our military representative, General Franklin Simian."

A massive, five-hundred-pound gorilla dressed in a tan shirt, camouflage shorts, and a beret stepped forward.

"Delighted to meet you, old chap," said the general, grasping Ian's hand firmly. "I would be most appreciative of a little chat over tea. I can think of a number of things we could discuss."

Ian stifled a yelp, as Simian's grip was like iron. "I'm sure there aaaregh," he gasped. "At your service, sir."

Hutch presented a chicken.

"Cluck, cluck, cluck," the chicken began.

Ether cleared his throat. "No fowl language please, Colonel. I'm pretty sure Ian doesn't speak it."

"Well o' course. What was ah thinking?" the chicken drawled. "The name's Sam—Sam Flanders. Ah am pleased to make yo' acquaintance. Ah hope you'll pahdon my rudeness just now, ah am accustomed to speaking with people who understand mah native tongue."

"Of course . . . uh, Colonel Flanders," Ian said, trying hard to smother a laugh. "Think nothing of it."

Hutch beamed at them all. "And we can't forget Heis. Heis?" he called. "Heis, are you here?"

"I'm not sure," said a voice to Ian's left. Ian jumped and looked around, seeing no one.

"This is a new friend of Ether's, Heis. His name is Ian, and he comes from the Other Side."

"A pleasure," the voice said from Ian's right. "I think."

"Where's Pixie?" Ether asked.

"She'll be around soon," Hutch said. "In the meantime, why don't we set up an impromptu committee lunch meeting? Set up a table out here?"

"Smashing idea," said the general. "Colonel, please assist me."

"Of course, sah."

* * *

THEY SET a large folding table out under a tree in front of the house and laid out tea, small sandwiches, cookies, and various other things to nibble. There was a brief moment of chaos when Ether tried to sit in the same corner as Simian and nearly broke the chair.

"I say, old man, no room," Simian grumbled.

"Sorry," Ether said. "Wasn't being careful about where I was going. I mean, there are cookies, after all, and I want to get some before Will sits down."

"I can never resist cookies," Will agreed.

"So, you didn't know you could visit my side or vice versa?" Ian was asking Hutch.

As Hutch turned to face him, Ian caught sight of a fierce blue script running the length of the inside of Hutch's ear. It read "Remember Caerbannog." He couldn't place the name but felt a healthy respect for the rabbit anyway, as a tattoo there looked painful.

"No, I had no idea," Hutch replied. He studiously avoided the carrot and celery sticks and picked up a cheese sandwich. "Actually, I was just about to call a meeting because the Origins Committee has been summoned to make a presentation to the Council of Archetypes."

Ether piled his plate high. "What for?"

"I guess the situation along the border is getting worse. The council wants to know if any of our research might help."

"Worse?" Ether raised an eyebrow. "What's going on?"

"A fine question," Simian nodded, sipping from a cup of tea. "Because you lot have been summoned before the council, I'm at liberty to tell you that a recent council study suggests that the Scourge has expanded to thirty-eight percent in the past year."

Ian was momentarily distracted by the sight of a sandwich floating off the table. It hovered for a moment, and half of it disappeared. Ian could hear chewing noises.

"Thirty-eight percent!" Ether swallowed hard. "That's at least ten times bigger than last year!"

"Quite so," said the general grimly. "It's accelerating. In addition, there are reports of battles breaking out in these areas. Most reports are unconfirmed, but they are surfacing with alarming frequency."

"Er," Ian said, raising a hand, "I'm lost. If you don't mind, what are you talking about?"

Ether looked apologetic. "I've been so busy pumping

him for information and giving him the grand tour that I haven't explained much about the actual structure of the Connectome beyond the basics, guys. You'll have to fill him in."

Hutch put his elbows on the table and steepled his paws. "You've been told where you are. Right, Ian?"

"More or less," Ian said. "Ether told me that this is what you call the Connectome, and you believe that things here are the products of the human imagination."

"Good," Hutch said. "But we can be more specific than that. This part of the Connectome is what we call Phantasmagoria. The other two major regions, according to the Theory of Connectome Structures, are the Complexus and the Badlands."

"Okay." Ian reached for a cookie and found only crumbs. He glanced at Ether, but the dragon was too busy wiping his mouth with the tablecloth to notice.

Hutch leaned back in his chair and adopted the pose of a serious but lop-eared lecturer. "In this portion of the Connectome, you'll generally find things like music, literary characters, jokes, and so forth. Things you might consider more fanciful."

"Whereahs," said the colonel, lighting up a thick cigar, which he clenched in his beak, "in the Technocity, which ah think Ether said you had visited, you'll find things like scientific concepts, mathematical equations, and all manner of gadgetry. So, for example, you'll find Einstein's Theory of Relations there."

"Relativity," Ian corrected automatically.

"Say again?" the chicken frowned.

"Einstein's Theory of Relativity. Einstein postulated that the inertia of a system increased as its velocity increased, such that all systems become infinitely heavy as the speed approaches that of light. This means that no system can surpass the velocity of light, because if a body has infinite mass, no force, however big, can accelerate it."

There was a confused silence. The chicken's beak worked as he tried repeating what Ian had just said to himself.

Ian looked around. "Sorry. Physics was a favourite subject in high school. How about: he said we can't go really, really, really fast?"

"Ahhhh," everyone said, looking relieved. There was a flurry of motion as notepads and pencils appeared all around. Ian peeked at Ether's pad. It read, "Einstein—not a genealogist."

"Right. So this is a little confusing because we were all over the place on our tour. But arts and humanities are clumped in one region—roughly speaking—and science, math, and engineering are in the other? And what, bad things in the Badlands?"

"Well done, ol' boy," said the general. "Got it in one."

"Lots of bad things." Ether nodded. "Everything humans consider evil, really. Demons, goblins, lawyers, ghosts, bankers, monsters, English literature essays, and zombies. There are also evil dragons, for that matter. Every villain—or evil concept—you guys have ever come up with."

"I suppose they all have to go somewhere," Ian mused. "I mean, if you guys are here and are products of our imagination, the other stuff has to show up here too."

"Yes," Will said hesitantly, "but it's not the Badlands that's the problem *per se*. Although it might be fuelling the problem. It's the Scourge."

"Which is . . .?"

"There's a darkness spreading along the border of the Technocity and the Badlands. And it's getting bigger. Faster than we thought possible."

"Thirty-eight percent bigger?"

"No, no." Ether shook his head. "It's expanded to thirty-eight percent of the Connectome. You see, Ian, the Connectome doesn't have definite boundaries like, say, your house does. You can't walk so many kilometres, find the edge, and drop off into space. As far as we know, the Connectome is infinite."

Ian tried to wrap his head around a concept like thirty-eight percent of infinity. He failed, and his mind snapped back into place painfully. "What causes it to expand?"

"We are not entirely sure." The gorilla removed his beret and picked lint off it carefully before replacing it. "We think it might be related to events on your side, but of course, that depends rather a lot on whether our basic theory of our origins is true to begin with. It has expanded before, many times, and shrunk again. When it gets bigger, there are numerous things that just . . . disappear. Ideas, inventions, concepts, stories. Once they get obscured by the Scourge, well, we've never seen them come back." Simian turned his sad eyes to Ian. "We're rather sure these scourge expansions are related to particularly bad times or regressive events. Things like libraries being destroyed, artworks smashed by invading armies, restrictions to freedom of expression, that kind of thing." Everyone around the table shivered. "How are things over there right now?"

Ian opened his mouth and shut it again. How to answer that? There wasn't a world war on (and all the attendant horrors those had brought with them). There wasn't a tense nuclear standoff between superpowers either—not like before. On balance, a lot of progress had been made on dozens of issues. But the last few years had definitely felt wrong...

"Iffy," Ian finally said. "There are days when it seems like we're going backwards fast. And the future is really uncertain."

The chicken let out a puff of fragrant smoke. "It feels the

same way heah," he said. "For a while, it felt easiah to contain the Scourge. Now, not as much."

"There's also the Creature," said Heis from somewhere underneath the table. "I think."

"Thank you for bringing that up, Heis," General Simian said. "That is the other troubling aspect of the increase. The speed of it seems related to the Creature. We've had reports of this thing for years, yet, we are still unsure as to how to stop it, nor do we even know much about it. That's why it has such a generic name. But it seems to be the central threat, the major force behind the current expansion of the Scourge."

"What will happen if the Scourge gets too big?" Ian's stomach fluttered, and he was suddenly aware of the tension around the table.

"It could wipe out everything," Ether said. "If we let it get out of control, that's the end of the Connectome. And, honestly, we're not sure how much power we have to hold back the tide if you guys keep pumping stuff in, you know?"

Everyone was quiet for a moment. Ether wiped watery eyes, and Ian was sure it wasn't entirely allergies making them well up.

"What are you going to do?" Ian said at last.

"First, we ah going to see what the council wants the Origins Committee to do," Flanders said. "Then we plan from theah."

"Ian, it looks like your arrival here might be really good luck," Ether said. "Not only can you help the committee, but you might be able to help the council too."

At that moment, General Simian stood up and gave a courtly bow in Ian's direction. "Pixie, my dear woman, how good of you to come."

Pixie, thought Ian, a tiny little character, perhaps in a

blouse and tutu, holding a wand. He turned around to see, looking down at ground level.

He looked up. And up. And up.

Pixie was tall. *Very* tall. She wore combat boots, camouflage pants, and an olive T-shirt, and her flaming red hair was pulled back into an efficient but loose knot. Her movements and demeanour were smooth and confident. Ian was utterly fascinated.

"No problem, General," Pixie said. "I have the Jabberwalk with me. I had a feeling the committee would want to carry a lot of notes with them."

Hutch clapped his paws together and rubbed them. "You're right. As much as I would love to sit around and chat some more, especially with Ian, we should get going. Let's clear this up and pack up some files."

"Quite so," Simian agreed. "Ian, would you care to join us?"

Ether reached over with his tail and gave Ian a sharp poke. Ian realized he'd been staring at Pixie.

"Wha? Oh. Ahem. Yes, General. I'm in. Definitely."

The group broke up and began clearing away the luncheon.

Ether leaned over and winked. "What's the matter? Haven't you ever seen a pixie before?"

"No." Ian shook his head. "She's not what I expected at all."

Ether nodded. "Tall, gorgeous, and she has a really great set of—"

"Ether!"

"—wings," said Ether firmly, pointing at Pixie's retreating figure. Sure enough, a pair of golden wings graced her back.

Ian was doubly enchanted. "Wow."

"Put it out of your mind," Ether admonished. "She's sweet on the general and nobody else."

Ian sighed and tore his gaze away. He focused on the dragon. "Ether, you look terrible. You really should take something for that."

Ether sniffed and nodded. "The object of your affection is wearing a distinctly floral scent today. It's making my nose itch like crazy, especially combined with all the pollen in this area, and Heis says he thinks he's out of medicine. I better nip home and meet you at the chambers."

"Come, sahs." The chicken marched past with a bucket under one wing. "We could use an extra pair of hands back heah."

They helped the colonel wash down the table and carried it back into the house. Then they started moving file boxes marked "Badlands" out of Heis's office into the front yard. Pixie moved what Ian assumed was the Jabberwalk into a position; it was a strange vehicle that looked like a dire wolf crossed with a battle mech, with flaming red headlights that eerily resembled eyes. The engine exhaust had a weird, musky smell.

Ian and Ether retrieved more boxes from Will and brought them outside. While Ether shoved one into the back of the Jabberwalk, Ian pulled the lid off one to peek inside. It had clearly not been disturbed for a while, as the top layer of papers was covered in dust. Curious, he picked up a sheet and blew it clean to read it.

"Hey, Ether, how old are these reports anyway?"

"Gnnk?"

Ian read the first paragraph. "Robin Hood," it said in what looked like Ether's handwriting. "Several versions, but the base model is green leotards, bows, and arrows. Good/evil? Unknown. Steals money but keeps trying to give it away." There was an asterisk and a footnote in another person's handwriting. "Connected to Boys in the Hood?" it asked.

Ian laughed. "You know, Ether, probably the smartest

thing for me would be to go through these systematically with you guys. It might save us a lot of time."

"Grdnk!"

Ian looked up. Ether was holding a talon tightly against his upper lip, and his eyelids were squeezed shut.

"Ether, do you need to sneeze?"

Suddenly, all activity around them ceased. In the silence, General Simian delicately cleared his throat. "Ether, my good fellow, did Ian just say you were going to sneeze?"

"GNNNK!" Ether quivered, waving his other claw madly in a shooing gesture. "Ah—"

"Ian, please step away from the dragon," Simian said urgently.

"Ah—"

Ian did not need to be told twice. He backed away as quickly as his legs would manage.

"AH—"

Pixie dived for cover underneath the Jabberwalk.

"AHHH—"

General Simian dropped his box of papers and threw himself behind a row of hedges. The chicken ducked.

"AHHHHH—"

"Okay. This is the last box," Hutch said as he stepped out of the house.

"CHOOOOOOOO!!!"

There was a brief local windstorm and a crackling sound. Then silence again.

"Much better," Ether snuffled.

Ian peered out from behind the lawn ornament that had become his temporary shelter. He expected to see an over-cooked pile of hasenpfeffer where Hutch used to be.

But Hutch was still there. His ears and fur were blown straight back, and his eyes were wide with terror. He still gripped the box tightly and had a slightly bluish tinge. He also glittered. In fact, everything around him did too.

"What the?" Ian said and walked up to the rabbit. "Hutch? Are you okay?" He reached out to shake him.

"Nonononono!" Pixie called out. She struggled out from underneath the Jabberwalk and jogged over. She pointed to a flower beside Hutch, which was also blue and sparkling. Pixie flicked it with a finger.

*Tnnngggg!*

*Tinkle.*

"Frozen solid," she pronounced, scuffing a boot over the shards.

Ether looked embarrassed. "I told you the barn fire wasn't on me, Ian. I breathe glitter, not fire. Freezing glitter."

"Oh my," Ian said, looking more closely at Hutch. "Rab*bits*."

"Exactly," Pixie said grimly. "Colonel, where did that pail of water go?"

The chicken came puffing up, sloshing water as he walked. "Ah am way ahead o' yoo," he clucked. He set a pail full of steaming water in front of Hutch. "Shall we?"

Ian watched as they gently pried Hutch's stiff form off the ground and lowered him into the water. Gradually, his ears drooped and his brown colour returned. He began shivering uncontrollably.

"Ah think, under the circumstances," Flanders said when Hutch's eyes began darting about, "it would be best if yoo stayed home, Hutch. Ah'm sure the council would undahstand."

It looked like Hutch shook his head no, but it was hard to tell with all the shivering. "N-n-nonsense," he said. "I'm chairman of the c-c-c-committee. I have to go. B-b-bring me a towel." Hutch made a supreme effort to stop shaking and levelled an icy glare at Ether. "And somebody get the dragon some allergy pills."

*  *  *

AFTER THEY HAD THAWED the rabbit and dosed the dragon, they all piled into the Jabberwalk. According to Pixie, it travelled at a top speed of twenty-five galumphs per hour. Ian couldn't tell whether this was fast or slow compared to dragon flight, as he was too busy trying to hold down his meal again. It moved in a fast, wavy, rocking motion that felt like a bad roller coaster ride. No one else seemed to mind; they all chatted amiably to each other or enjoyed the swaying scenery.

Shortly after they left Heis's house, Hutch sneezed. It wasn't a tornado-inducing cold front of glitter like Ether's had been, but a rather cute, apologetic explosion.

*"Choo!"*

With the delicate sneeze, damp towel, and drooping ears, Ian thought Hutch looked adorable in a pathetic sort of way. Hutch caught him looking.

"Say what you're thinking, and I swear I will chew your ankles *right off*," he muttered.

Ian carefully sidled away.

Sometime later, the Jabberwalk pulled up in front of a vast set of grey, windowless, monolithic buildings that seemed to stretch up and out as far as the eye could see. Ian staggered out of the Jabberwalk, put his hands on his knees, and focused on breathing deeply. He'd had no idea that he was so prone to travel sickness.

Simian leaped cheerfully out of the vehicle and gave Ian a solid thump on the back. "Chin up there, old man. You'll get used to it in no time. Help us get unloaded."

Ian walked unsteadily over to help remove the boxes of

paper, this time careful about where the dust was. "Where is this?"

"Bureaucracy Prime," Hutch replied and then blew his nose so hard that his ears stuck straight back and his tail stiffened. "Everyone have Every Possible Document That Might Be Required?"

There was much patting of pockets and nodding as thick sheaves of papers were produced. "What will we do about Ian?" Ether asked.

Simian had the look of someone who was preparing for a major battle. "I dare say they're unlikely to have regulations on non-Connectome residents. No one even knew bringing one here was even possible until this week."

Pixie did a headcount, saw that everyone was ready, and nodded. "Lock and load, people. Let's do this."

Ian, wondering what he was in for this time, followed them into the largest building. They stopped in front of an enormous directory sign. "Where are the council chambers today, Pixie?" Simian asked.

"Today?" Ian was puzzled. "Do they move or something?"

"All the time," Simian replied. "Law of Inexplicable Policy Changes."

"Aw jeez," Pixie said. "It's bad, guys. We'll have to run the whole gauntlet today. The first part isn't so bad; it's just the usual quicksand traps and lava floors."

"Quicksand?" Ian exclaimed. "What's that doing inside a building?"

"Eh?" Ether said. "Why wouldn't it be? People on your side have to rescue nearly everything from the stuff, as far as we can tell. Little blue people, talking cars, macho soldiers . . ."

"But—"

"And then," Pixie continued grimly, "we have to get past all *three* Clerk Types."

Everyone moaned.

In the morose silence that followed, Ian said, "Dare I even ask?"

Simian sighed. "Pissy Clerk on a Power Trip, New Guy Who Knows Nothing, and Clerk Two Days Out From Retirement Who Doesn't Give a—"

Ian held up a hand. "Got it. Did we bring rations?"

Ether looked surprised. "You've done this before, haven't you?"

* * *

THE EXHAUSTED GROUP walked slowly into Waiting Room 21b. Pixie's trousers were coated in fine, damp sand up to her thighs. Hutch's tail was still smouldering. Ether sported a date stamp on his forehead, and Flanders had taken several "Sign Here —>" sticky-note shots to the chest.

Simian girded his everything and walked up to the enormous reception booth at the front of the room. It was entirely enclosed in safety glass. There were three small holes at eye level and a slide-through slot on the desk. A sign taped to the glass proclaimed "RUDE PATRONS WILL BE DEALT WITH SEVERELY."

"Good day, madam. I—"

The woman inside the booth rolled her eyes and pointed left. There was a small machine for dispensing numbered papers. Simian was nonplussed for a moment, as the room was empty save for their party. A veteran of several campaigns through Bureaucracy Prime, he recovered quickly and took a number. It read "21."

Just then, there was a quiet *ping* from a digital counter near the ceiling. It read "4." Simian's normally ramrod-straight posture wilted ever so slightly. He came back to the group with a very stiff upper lip. "Right. Who's got some playing cards?"

Ian had learned six new games by the time their number finally came up. Bored and sore from sitting on the hard waiting room chairs, he followed Simian up to the booth.

"Good day, madam. We are here to attend the council meeting."

The woman in the booth pivoted in her chair to face them. "You'll need miafihto aiidhgil awiuti and of course kjslkdi maiwlld jdkkdk fiohjgjjt and—"

Frowning, Simian said, "Madam, could you repeat that? I'm afraid—"

The woman looked pointedly at the back of the rude-patrons sign. She moved her hand slowly over to a group of three big red buttons on her desk. Ian risked a peek over Simian's shoulder. The first button was labelled "Open Trap Door."

"I assure you, madam," Simian said quickly, "I was not trying to be cheeky—"

She moved her hand a bit more to hover over a button labelled "Summon Rhinos."

Simian whipped off his beret in supplication. "It's just that this," he gently and very politely tapped the glass, "makes it hard to hear you."

The woman lowered her hand. Ian held his breath. She pressed the third button, marked "Microphone On."

"You'll need to fill out Form 435d, Form UDHH, extended version, and have you got an import licence for that?" She pointed at Ian.

"Er, import licence? I didn't think that—"

She silenced him with a dead-eyed look. "The Connectome Border Act, Section 12, Paragraph 8, Subparagraph ix. You must have a licence to import humoons into the Connectome."

"Humans," Ian said automatically. Simian slid a foot over to step slowly but firmly on his. Five hundred pounds of gorilla wasn't kidding. Ian let out a whimper to acknowledge that the message had been received.

"Is there a form for this as well?" Simian asked, the grip on his beret tightening noticeably.

Waves of indifference rolled off the clerk. She reached into a filing cabinet and pulled out a ginormous form. Ian reckoned it was at least forty pages. She slid it through the slot in the glass. "Remember to take a number when you're done."

Beads of sweat appeared on Simian's forehead. "Jolly good. I don't suppose you've some spare pens? It's only that we went through—"

The woman's hand moved back to hovering over the rhinos button.

"No? That's just fine then. We'll be back in a jiffy."

* * *

BY THE TIME they made it to the chambers, Simian's writing arm was in a sling and he'd developed a tic in his left cheek. They made themselves comfortable in the delegation gallery.

The Council of Archetypes chambers were official-looking in a medieval sort of way. There was a grand entryway—all red carpet and dark wood— that smelled pleasantly of polish. The meeting room itself was large, with a vaulted ceiling and the obligatory marble and granite accents and carved pillars. The councillors sat at a massive wood table with legs carved in the shape of animal limbs. They were so lifelike that Ian swore he could see them moving from time to time.

"It's a good thing we finally got in here," Ian whispered to Ether, who had wedged his dragon butt into a chair beside him. "I thought after all those delays, we'd miss the meeting."

"Oh, there was never any chance of that. These things go on forever." He pulled out a pencil and a card with a five-by-five grid marked on it.

Ian laughed, but after a while, it became apparent that Ether hadn't been kidding. These councillors droned on longer than the ones at home did. He studied the various members of the council. Given the name, he'd been expecting it to have something like a hero, a crone, or a jester.

"So, like, what are you going to do about thith water drainage problem thingy on the weth bank?" said a young woman with a pronounced lisp. Her nameplate identified her as Babs. She wore a form-fitting cashmere sweater, had her blonde hair done up in a bouffant, and there was a nail file on the desk in front of her. She snapped the gum she was chewing, and the sound echoed in the chamber.

Ian frowned. Seeing his face, Ether nudged him and pointed to an information packet crammed into a pocket on the back of the chair in front of him. It was titled *A History of Your Council: An Infinity of Serving YOU*, and Ian began thumbing through it. On page fifty, he learned that the organization had once been known as the Council of Bad Stock Characters and Stereotypes and that it had been "shortened" to Archetypes as part of a supposed plain-language-in-government campaign. Ian noted with amusement that the name change had happened at roughly the same time Ether had said that they'd started observing the human world. The council had clearly rebranded to improve its image.

He returned his attention to the council. Other members included a middle-aged woman with short-cropped grey hair, whom Ian pegged as Formidable Older Woman, a bulbous-headed, rubbery creature with almond-shaped eyes named Ne'ila, an arrogant male deity calling himself Adonis, an older man whom Ian had already noted had a habit of saying absolutely nothing at length, a unicorn, and a young man in a plaid shirt, knit cap, and tan boots, whose name-plate said simply "Joe."

The water issue Babs had mentioned dragged on for another half an hour. Ian leaned over to Ether. "These are the wise guys that your military puts so much faith in? They dither more than any council I've ever attended!"

"Wise guys? You mean Vinnie and Guido? They're not on the council," Ether replied.

"Never mind."

At last, Formidable Older Woman, whose name turned out to be Hagar, stood up and called for a vote. When the motion passed, she gestured at the delegation. "You can come forward now," she said. "And your little dog too."

"Dog?!" Hutch sputtered and then sneezed.

"You'll have to forgive Hagar, Hutch," Adonis said in a booming, godly voice that made Ian want to cover his ears. "She is new to the council and not yet aware of your position with the committee."

"Er, yes, Lady Hagar," Ether said. "Hutch would be the chair of the committee."

Hagar gave Ether a glare that was clearly the withering I-Raised-Six-Children-Alone-With-One-Hand-Tied-Behind-My-Back-So-I-Don't-Give-A-Crap-About-Your-Delicate-Sensibilities glare. Ian shivered, remembering that same look from his sixth-grade school librarian.

Ether laid a restraining hand on Hutch's shoulder. "Ah, okay. Well, how can the committee be of service to the council?"

The older man made to stand up, but Adonis waved him down and said, "As I'm sure General Simian has told you, there's increased activity in the Badlands. The size of it is increasing, and we've received a number of reports of *coordinated* attacks by villainous characters." He glanced down at the table. "This is a rather unwelcome development, as they've never been particularly well organized before. Today's involved numerous Men with Pointy Teeth and Bad Hair."

"Vampires," Ian said.

Adonis looked amused. "And who is this puny thing?"

Hutch, whiskers still twitching, introduced him. "This is Ian, Lord Adonis. We procured him from the Other Side as part of our special and capital projects expenditures this year."

The rest of the committee looked a bit startled at this.

"The Other Thide?" Babs squealed. "Omigawd! All that budget stuff we talked about was, like, totally justified?"

"Of course, Lady Babs," Hutch said. "I certainly wouldn't go so far as to suggest that we anticipated the rise in incidents along the Badlands, but we certainly believed that the expertise from someone on the Other Side would help Origin studies immensely."

Hagar snickered. "Pretty smooth for a rodent."

Hutch's ears went rigid.

The older man seized the opportunity to stand up again and grasp his lapels. "I don't have a question, so much as a comment..."

"Yes! Bingo!" Ether said, marking something on his grid.

"I sah, Ether, that's your second win this month," Flanders muttered.

The man droned on, undeterred. "I would like to express this council's gratitude for the committee's astonishing initiative. This day will go down in the Connectome's history as a pivotal—"

"ghe'torDaq luSpet 'oH DaqlIj'e'!" said Ne'ila, and she

made an obviously rude gesture. The man turned bright red and sat down abruptly.

"What did the alien say?" Ian asked Ether.

"I'm not completely sure," the dragon said, looking embarrassed. "But the sign she made has something to do with asking the unicorn to put his horn someplace delicate if he didn't sit down and be quiet."

Adonis drummed his fingers on the table, and little sparks flew away from his fingertips. "You were saying, Ian?"

"Um," Ian said, trying to remember the question. "Vampires. I think you mean vampires."

"How do we get rid of vampires?"

"Let's see," Ian ticked the methods off on his hand. "Silver crosses, a stake through the heart, and garlic, I believe."

Adonis nodded to the unicorn. "Remind me to order extra steaks and garlic for the military ration packs."

"But—" Ian started to say when Joe interrupted.

"Well, that's great, eh? Bud what air we gonna do aboot the Creature? We can go oot an' fight all these vampires, eh? Bud that doesn't deal with the big fella. He seems to be the leader, eh?"

The older man shot up but, after a sharp glance from Ne'ila, refrained from grabbing his lapels. "I agree with Lord Joe in principle, but I believe I am duty-bound to remind council that we don't have much information about the Creature. Our reconnaissance scouts have not been able to get past the Creature's minions, about which they also know very little."

"Yes, well," Hutch said, gesturing at the boxes of files. "We have—"

"I said steak, not mignon," muttered Adonis. "Let's try to stay on budget this year, okay?"

"So, like, you're thaying that every time scouths go into the Badlands, they run into a new threat?" Babs asked.

The older man nodded. "If they survive an encounter, they usually find that discretion is the better part of valour, and they come back to file a report."

Hagar grumbled. "You mean they turn tail and run."

"Put whatever spin on it you like, Hagar." Adonis stretched in his chair. "At the end of the day, it means we're still only getting information in dribs and drabs."

"Yes, so," Hutch tried again, "we have been studying—"

"You wouldn't be if you'd send *female* scouts," Hagar said not quite under her breath.

"You know my position on sending women into combat situations," Adonis said in a tone that implied that this was a familiar argument.

Babs rolled her eyes. "You are *thuch* a mythogynist."

"Ahem!" Hutch squeaked, surreptitiously wiping his increasingly pink nose. "So, what exactly can the Origins Committee do to help? We do have files on Badlands occupants that we would be happy to turn over to the council and the military, and we'd be willing to help review information from the scout reports and—"

"I been thinkin', eh?" Joe said. "Sorry, but Ian has awready pointed oot that the scout descriptions of the vampire were off, right? So, how accurate are the other reports?"

Hagar nodded and added, "Especially if they're made on the run."

Joe cleared his throat. "Lookit, my point is that we're expecting the committee to make sense of second-hand reports that might be way off, okay? Sorry, but I think we should send the whole committee into the Badlands to get accurate first-hand accoonts."

There was a long silence. This, Ian thought, would be the one thing they would all agree on.

On cue, Adonis said, "All in favour?"

"Aye."

"Yeah, eh?"

"I do believe this is something I can support, as it conforms to my belief—"

"Heghlu'meH QaQ jajvam."

"Neigh."

Adonis glared at the unicorn. "Misty, I've asked you before to clop your hooves for votes. As the councillor in charge of legislative discipline—"

"Oooh, watch him whip," Hagar said sarcastically.

"—I need clarity," Adonis grated. "Is that a *yay* neigh or a *nay* neigh?"

Misty made a rude noise and a rainbow appeared.

"Fine. Motion carried. I move to recess."

"But—" Ether waved ineffectually.

The councillors filed out. "Poor thing. I hope your cold geth better thoon. Although you do look cute with your pink nose."

Ether pulled Hutch back just in time. His teeth made a nasty snapping noise in the empty air where Babs' ankle had been.

The committee members sat there, looking at each other in stunned silence.

"So, now what do we do?" Ether asked.

"I'm not certain," Heis replied.

* * *

THE TRIP BACK TO HEIS' house was quiet.

"Well, gentlemen," the colonel said as they arrived, "I do declah that theah is nothin' else for it but to plan our reconnaissance mission."

Simian nodded. "Agreed."

"Ah shall go arrange for support staff, sah." Flanders disappeared into the house.

"Darn!" Ether slapped a claw to his forehead. "Did anyone think to get a Quest Permit from the Clerk's Office? I really don't want to have to run the gauntlet again."

"Way ahead of you." Pixie waved a fistful of paperwork. "I stepped out during the council meeting and got it. And Weapons Permits, Intelligence Gathering Authorizations, Transportation of Food across Established Connectome Borders, and of course the Permits to Hold Permits and Authorizations. Oh and Permission to Travel in the Company of an Other Sider." She smiled dazzlingly at Ian. "The clerk made that one up just for you."

"The clerk can do that? Doesn't the council have to debate it or something to make new procedures?"

"Wow!" Pixie shook her head in wonder. "You really are from the Other Side. Do elected officials there actually have any say in day-to-day policy?"

Ian thought about it for a moment. "No, I suppose not."

"I d-d-don't mean to intrude," said Will, who had been hovering in the background the whole time, "but I mean, shouldn't we get on with the preparation montage?"

"Will's right," Pixie said, clapping her hands. "General? Should we go get provisions?"

"Capital idea." He proffered an arm, and they set off toward the Jabberwalk.

"Hutch, do you want us to investigate anything in particular while we're in the Badlands?" Ether asked.

"I'm combing alongg."

"Hutch, you're sick," Ether scolded.

"I am not going to biss this because I hab a cold. Or are you imblying I'b a wimp? Dat I'b too soft for dis?"

"Nonono." Ether backed away carefully.

"Good. Heis, are you combing?"

"I guess so," Heis replied from underneath Ether's tail.

"Good. He'll be able get a supply of nodebooks. Where's Will?"

Silence.

"Mr. Power?" More silence. "Anyone know where he's gone?" No one did. "Figures," Hutch grumbled. "Always vanishing when you need him."

*  *  *

ABOUT AN HOUR LATER, they all gathered in Heis' front yard again.

Looking at the ragtag crew, Ian could barely suppress a laugh. Pixie and the general had returned with their support staff in tow. Dressed in red shirts, black pants, and black boots, they answered to the names Lieutenant Nebbish, Sergeant Bane, and Private Hemloch. They'd brought rations, backpacks, an array of swords and daggers, and clothing.

Ether had turned a long black belt into a headband and was carefully daubing his glistening pink scales with splotches of green and black camo paint. Hutch had pulled on a pair of combat boots and camo pants. He wore little black bands around his upper arms and studded black wrist braces. He had also oiled his chest. Will was finally spotted slinking around the supplies in a set of bland, tan fatigues, while Heis, of course, was unsure where he was or what he was doing.

Pixie stopped in front of Ian and looked him over. He'd chosen a simple green combat tunic, green pants, and sturdy boots. "So many pockets," she sighed and moved on to her next task.

Ian looked down. It was true: the trousers had more than he knew what to do with. He picked up his backpack and pulled it on. "Ooof," he said. "Tell me again why we can't just galumph in, take a few notes, and come back? Or fly? Pixie's a pilot, right?"

Simian tsked. "Not standard operating procedure for situations like this. A quest *must* be done on foot, through difficult terrain, bad weather, and dark and creepy places at some point. Oh, and a lot of talk about food."

"Why?"

Ether stopped painting his belly button to think about that. "No idea, now that you mention it. We've always done it that way. Old hobbits are hard to break, I guess."

"Oy." Ian pinched the bridge of his nose.

"May ah suggest, General, that we swing through the Complexus to stop at R's lab to pick up our Cool Gadgets?"

"You read my mind, Colonel. Everyone ready? Forward ho!"

They set off, Pixie and the colonel in the front and the three red shirts and Will taking up the rear. Everyone else crowded around Ether in the middle.

"Ow! That's my tail!"

"Sorry."

"Choo!"

"Bless you."

"Hey, watch where you're putting that sword!"

"Didn't mean it, old chap."

"I don't mean to sound pushy or anything, but did anyone remember to turn out the lights before we left?"

"I'm not certain."

"Argh! Now I've broken a talon. I hate it when I do that!"

"It's not broken, Ether—only chipped."

"Are we there yet?"

"Ask that again, and I swear I'll turn this expedition right around."

"Choo!"

"Alright, alright." Ether stopped in his tracks, and

inevitably, everyone behind him crashed into his back end. As several of them carried sharp objects, it was a moment before his eyes stopped watering and he could ungrit his teeth. "Could we *please* spread out? I'm a free-range dragon. I need my personal space."

"Dis dose not bode well for de rest of de twip," Hutch sniffled. "Why are we having so bany pwoblems alweady? Did we biss a step?"

Pixie pulled out a clipboard and ticked off items on a list. "Permits, montage, first stop chosen . . . Aha! You're right, Hutch. We forgot to synchronize our watches."

"Ah," Hutch nodded.

Everyone pulled out their timekeeping devices. It was a bizarre assortment of miniature sundials, hourglasses, pocket watches, and Ian's phone. A brief but heated argument broke out between Will and Heis about the uncertain nature of man's perception of time.

Once Pixie had pulled them apart, she ticked off the final item on their checklist.

"Forward again!" The general pointed inspirationally.

They walked until dusk, going past the meadow and pushing into a forest before making camp in a clearing. Flanders passed out some packages labelled "Meticulously Researched Edibles," and they all tucked into their dinners. Afterward, Hutch took a jar out of his backpack and began smearing oil on his chest again. Simian's nostrils flared slightly.

"Hutch, comrade, that oil you have on your chest?"

"Yes?"

"Very masculine, I thought. Rather a nice touch, actually."

"Yes?"

"It's just that . . . well, it smells rather—"

"If you mean to imbly that it's mentholated, I will hab to chew your ankles off. Real rabbits don't neeb medicine."

"Ah. Quite so."

They settled in for the night, Ether bunking down beside Ian. "Well?" he asked. "What do you think of Phantasmagoria so far?"

"It's . . . different," Ian said.

"I wouldn't live anywhere else in the Connectome." Ether appeared not to notice Ian's lack of enthusiasm. "Wouldn't want to live in the Complexus. I mean, you saw the capital city; it's *weird* there."

Ian glanced over at a tree stump, where he spotted a sleepy swarm of bees stitching a quilt. "Yes, it sure is."

They were quiet for a while, enjoying the crackle of the fire and the low murmur of discussions elsewhere in the campsite. Ether stretched out onto his back, his back feet sticking straight up, his front claws clasped behind his head.

"Ian?"

"Mmm?"

"Ian?"

"M-what?"

"You're staring again."

"Huh? Oh." Ian shook himself. He had been staring across the camp at Pixie, who was deep in conversation with Simian. They were looking over maps and lists and gazing adoringly into each other's eyes.

Ian sighed and lay back beside Ether to stare up at the stars. "Why do we always want the things we can't have?"

Ether shrugged. "I don't know. Maybe we want the wrong things? Like, say, you wanting to leave Teisburg, for example."

There was a pregnant pause.

"Ether," Ian finally gave birth to a sentence. "Is this you trying to do the male bonding thing again? Because I was kind of being rhetorical just now."

"Well, we are two guys sitting around a campfire. All we need is a six-pack."

"You drink?"

"Six-packs are for drinking?"

Ian laughed. "Yes. It refers to six beers. What did you think you did with them?"

"No clue. It seems to go hand in hand with guys and fires, according to your movies."

"Not if you want to have *intelligent* conversations, you don't. I mean, the only way to make the night even dumber would be to start rolling joints."

"Spraining things deliberately would be pretty dumb." Ether rolled over on his side, propped himself up on his elbow, and winked at Ian. "So, what do you like best about her? Her eyes? Her legs?"

"Ugh, Ether. Seriously? What's with all the 'bro' dragon stuff? There's way more to a woman than the way she looks. She seems smart, she's confident, and she's very good at what she does. I'd love to be able to settle down with someone like that."

"And why don't you like Teisburg?"

Ian puffed out his cheeks in frustration. "You're not going to let that go, are you? Fine. I've lived in small towns all my life. I want to *do* something important. Be where the action is. Plus, I'm not getting far in my next game story. Teisburg stuff keeps getting in the way."

"How much do you have finished?"

Ian yawned suddenly and stretched. "Don't you think we should be getting some sleep? Tomorrow's a big day." He closed his eyes.

"Oh no you don't." Ether leaned over and delicately prised his eyes open. Ian found himself staring up into a gigantic dragon visage. "Tomorrow will be the same size as today.

Don't try to change the subject. How much of this game have you finished so far?"

Ian struggled to close his eyes, but Ether just loomed closer, making his eyes puddle up as he tried to focus. He gave up.

"Nothing," he mumbled.

"Nothing?" Ether was incredulous as he let go. "Not even an outline?"

"I don't even have a concept." Ian heaved another sigh. "I haven't been able to do anything . . . well, since I did my last game. I don't know why."

Ether's brows knit together. "Did the game not do well? Is that it? Fear of failure?"

"Far from it. Bestseller. All kinds of popular merchandise made about it. I think it got optioned for a movie too."

"Wow!"

"Yeah, wow. But I didn't see a dime of any of that. The company I worked for merged, I was made redundant, and well, here I am. Well, not *here*. I mean, that's how I ended up in Teisburg. Couldn't find work anywhere else, and I have student loans like you wouldn't believe."

"So what—" Ether began, but a movement overhead caught his attention. A majestic red dragon glided over the canopy of trees and disappeared from view.

Ether practically melted.

Ian could almost see the little hearts floating above his head. "That was her, wasn't it?" he said. "Ginger."

"Uh-huh." Ether drew in a deep breath and let it out slowly, his lower lip quivering as he exhaled. "Talk about wanting something you can't have."

Ian nudged him, bruising his elbow in the process. "How do you know you can't have her? Have you ever asked? Is she seeing another dragon?"

"Pfft," Ether snorted, waving a talon dismissively. "She'd

take one look at me and laugh me out of her apartment. I'm *pink*. I blow glitter, Ian."

"So?"

"Do you know how many times I've been teased about that?"

"When?"

"All the time."

"Lately?"

"Well no, but—"

"When was the last time? A year . . . two years ago?"

"No."

"So, when?"

Ether blinked. "When I was a dragonlet, I suppose. They used to laugh and call me names. I was never invited to play any dragon games either."

"Annnnd basically, you're telling me you've let a bunch of dorky kids' comments inform your perceptions of dragon masculinity?"

Ether stared at him for a moment and then yawned hugely. "Say, you're right. It's getting late. Time for some shut-eye." He curled up into a ball and closed his eyes.

Ian reached over to try to pry his eyelids open. Nothing budged. He tried both hands. Nary a flicker.

"Eyelids of steel, my friend." Ether smirked. "Go to sleep."

Ian chuckled, propped himself up against Ether's side, pulled out his notepad, and started jotting down the day's events. He was still hoping that everything he saw here would gel into something he could use to get writing again.

* * *

WHEN THEY WOKE UP, it was a bright, clear, and sunny day. Ian began to think he could enjoy this questing business.

*Thump!*

"What the heck was that noise?"

Ether sucked on a talon and waved it in the air, nodding wisely. "Temperature just fell."

Overhearing, Pixie pulled out her clipboard and scanned her quest checklist. "Weather," she said, ticking the box, "Starts Turning for the Worst. We're on schedule, people, but we won't stay that way for long if we don't hustle. Come on, move it, move it."

Ian felt a chill in the air and buttoned up his tunic. He watched in admiration as Flanders broke down his camp area and packed it away with smooth efficiency. "The colonel seems like a seasoned campaigner," Ian remarked.

"Should be," Ether agreed. "He's been doing it for eleven years that I know of."

They cleared away any traces of their camp and marched away into the bright dawn. The air became increasingly cool, but the sky stayed a brilliant blue. About mid-morning, they broke through the forest and found themselves staring at a valley full of green pastures and neat gardens.

"I am dot complaining," said Hutch, "because dat would be soft and wabbit-like." Everyone solemnly agreed while unconsciously rubbing their ankles. "But shouldn't we be in Complexus by now? With all dis marching?"

"We've been tacking Fluxward to minimize the amount of Complexus we'll have to cross to get to the Badlands." Pixie pulled out a map. "But let me check where we are."

While everyone else eased their packs off and sat down for a rest, Ian stepped closer to peer over Pixie's shoulder.

He had to rub his eyes: the map seemed... *alive*. The rivers weren't just meandering blue lines; actual streams of water flowed along the page. Hills stood up as bumps and valleys were dimples on the surface. The borderline between Phantasmagoria and Complexus writhed gently, alternately excluding and including a big red dot that was labelled 'You Are Here.'

"Whoa," said Ian, slack-jawed.

Pixie jumped, unaware she had an audience. "Hey, you shouldn't be looking at this! It's classified."

"Then how come you have it? I thought you were freelance?"

"Umm…" Pixie turned slightly pink. She flexed her wings nervously and carefully avoided looking over at General Simian.

Ian grinned. "Just tell me what I'm not seeing."

"You absolutely didn't see a VRML map, which doesn't stand for Very Real Map Language, and it surely doesn't have anything to do with cutting-edge positioning technology based on a new understanding of the space-time continuum, because the military certainly wouldn't be using council money to research such a thing. Also, tachyons." Pixie looked at him hopefully.

"Ah," he said. "Gosh, that sun is so bright. I can hardly see for the glare."

Pixie relaxed and patted his shoulder gratefully. "We should be right on the border, according to this ancient and outdated map I have here," she said to the rest of the group.

"What do you think, Heis? Can you fly up and see where we are?"

"I'm not sure where *I* am," Heis replied.

"Ah believe we ah on track, mah compatriots. Look yonder at the patch to our immediate right."

It was a neat orchard of trees. The leaves were oval and leathery-looking, while the fruits were green and teardrop-shaped. And growing in a remarkable pattern.

Ian squinted. They spelled out:

$$6.02252 \times 10^{23}$$

"HOLY GUACAMOLE," Ether said. "I think I know where I am now. There's a group of mols that live here along the border."

They pushed farther into the valley, passing carefully tended fields and tussocky pastures.

"Guys, guys," Pixie said in a hushed voice. "Isn't that Socowtes, the Greek philosopher?"

"*The* Socowtes?" Ether asked. "Where?" He followed Pixie's gaze. A bull sat on his backside, quietly asking questions of a group of intense young calves.

They walked by the group in awed and respectful silence. Socowtes paused and nodded politely in their direction.

"$\mu$," he said.

They broke into excited gabbling when they were far enough away.

"Ah must say, it is not evahry day you are acknowledged by one of the greatest thinkers of the world," the colonel remarked.

"Indeed, Colonel," the general beamed. "One for the journal tonight, I should think."

"This . . . isn't what I was expecting," Ian said. "I figured the entire Complexus would be things like the gleaming towers and scientific theorems and so on."

"Most of that is in the cities. We're walking along the border at the moment, and it's not a hard dividing line," Ether explained. "Along this sort of fuzzy edge, you'll find things that might be part of science and philosophy but that have also taken on a semi-mythical status amongst your kind. And don't forget, technology isn't just your phone. When you humans first picked up a stick and sharpened it, it became a tool . . . a kind of technology. Some of the Connectome's most fascinating things live in this area: ideas, theories, inventions, and discoveries right alongside some of your most interesting bits of culture, literature, and philosophy. This convergence of your arts and sciences is one of Will's favourite places to study. Heis loves it too. Isn't that right, Heis?"

Silence.

"Darn. We've lost him. He's probably off listening to the philosopher."

Ian laughed suddenly, the fresh air and exercise making him feel better than he had in a long time. "In search of bovine inspiration, you mean."

Ether's eyes twinkled in return. "Not bad, not bad. You mootilated the delivery though."

"Ha! I knew I could cownt on you to milk an opening."

Ether put both claws to his chest, pretending to be wounded. "Two shots in one! You win this round."

Ian grinned triumphantly but then wondered whether it was a win or a loss. He was beginning to think in bad puns, after all.

"If you two are quite through," Pixie said, calling back to them, "I'd like to be on an approach vector to the Badlands by dusk, and we still have one more stop scheduled. Get the lead out."

Ian gave her a respectful but casual salute. "Yes, ma'am," he said and walked faster.

\* \* \*

THEY APPROACHED the outskirts of another future city. Their stop turned out to be a small, nondescript laboratory facility tucked away in a funky suburb composed of Dymaxion houses and geodesic domes. They waited in the lobby until a short, stocky man with a shock of red tufty hair who was wearing a lab coat buzzed them in.

"Welcome, welcome," he said. "We don't often get visitors. And, I, uh, hardly leave."

"Pleasure to be here, R," said Simian. "What sort of gadgets can you set us up with today? We're going on a reconnaissance mission."

"Oh!" He raised a finger. "I love outfitting missions. Follow me."

He led them past a group of boring desks and standard cubicles and pressed a hidden button in the back wall. A secret door swung open to reveal a gleaming high-security elevator. R punched in an access code and followed them in.

The elevator took a long time to descend; Ian could feel his eardrums popping. The doors opened to a state-of-the-art facility bustling with technonerds going about their business.

Ian gaped. Everything looked so cool.

R took them into a large demonstration room lined on all four walls with strange devices. "So," he tapped his chin, "reconnaissance mission. Exploding pen?"

"Er, no," said Simian.

"Exploding teacup?"

"No, thank you. I take my tea black, not splattered."

"Eyeglasses where the lenses can be turned into spinning blades of death? Laser shoelaces? Necktie that doubles as a garrote? Er, wait, I think we had trouble with the prototype on that one…"

Simian ground his teeth a little. "No weapons as such, R. We need cameras, transceivers, that sort of thing."

"Oh." R's shoulders slumped. "How boring."

"What's this do?" Will picked up a briefcase.

*Fzzzzzzt.*

R brightened. "Oh, yes. That's a favourite. Electrified hand luggage. Excellent booby trap."

Will smouldered gently.

"But," R continued sadly, "you want cameras. I don't suppose you'll be in the quantum realm?" He picked up a detection wand and waved it around. All of a sudden, they could see a solitary figure standing in the centre of the room, buck naked except for a pair of undershorts with bright-red kissy lips all over it.

Ether cleared his throat. "Heis, we've talked about this. You *really* need to put on pants before we leave the house. Just in case."

"Oh my." R blushed and turned off the wand. "Ahem. Moving on. Ah, here we go. Cameras. Long range, short range, infrared, dark-matter detection . . ."

"You can do that?" Ian blurted out.

"Pfft." R waved him off. "Easy peasy. Did that years ago. Now, getting a clear shot of a thief in a convenience store . . . *that* will be my greatest triumph."

Pixie made some impatient coughing noises.

"We'll be pleased to acquire all of your cameras," Simian said. "And long-range communications equipment. Transmitters. Sensors. The works."

"Knock yourselves out!" R stepped back to let them pull things off the wall. "You sure you don't want any explody things, though? I've got a great new line of illudium—"

"No explosions," Simian said firmly. "Not today."

R sighed.

* * *

THEY LEFT R's lab and went back out on the road. It had gotten even colder. On the horizon, a bank of ominous clouds was growing. The land ahead was dark and shadowed.

Ian began to feel uneasy. He looked over his shoulder frequently as they walked.

They marched steadily along a rough trail for an hour in relative silence, with only the occasional curse or exclamation when someone stumbled over a rock in the increasing gloom. Suddenly, Simian pulled them to a halt and wandered over to a field that had clearly once been a lush and fertile crop of wheat. He picked a bunch and brought them over; they crowded around him to look. The heads were yellow and blighted with black spots that smelled like mould. The stems were withered and broken in several places.

Hutch looked bilious. Pixie averted her eyes.

Ian was puzzled. "This is just crop damage, right?"

"No, Ian," Simian said sadly. "This is the edge of where the Badlands darkness has spread. This is no ordinary crop damage. This was deliberate. We're dealing with cereal killers here."

\* \* \*

THEY PUSHED DEEPER into the Badlands. The landscape became even more despoiled. Low-lying areas were flooded with dank, putrid water. They passed dead animals, insects, and birds—piles and piles of them—as they marched. The weather became wildly unpredictable: cold and still one minute, then baking hot and gale-force winds the next. By the time they found a safe place to camp in a semi-sheltered outcropping at the top of a hill, they were battered, bruised, and exhausted.

Pixie set about making a fire, while everyone else moved to store their gear in a dry spot under the rock ledge. Simian had taken out some binoculars and scanned the trail ahead.

"Look lively," he said after a minute. "I rather believe we have incoming."

Ian came over to see, and Simian handed over the binoculars. Some distance away, a lone figure was pelting down the trail toward them. "One of the scouts the council was talking about?"

Simian nodded. "My thought as well. Probably don't have to worry about him, but I am rather concerned about what's making him run so hard."

They waited tensely for his arrival, alternately tracking him and scanning the area behind him. Finally, he burst into their campsite.

"We've lost!" he wailed and collapsed.

"Phil?" Flanders said, bending over the man's body. "Is that you?"

His chest heaved up and down as he sucked in air. "I've been running for twenty-six . . ." He paused, grasping the bottle of water someone offered him and gulping at it greedily. "I have information."

They propped him up and waited while he caught his breath. "The Creature," he said at last. "The Creature is behind all of this." He waved at the landscape. "The spread of it. The weather. And it's recruiting. It's bringing out the worst of everything. Everything, I say!" He pulled at Flanders's wing, drawing himself up painfully. "There's an advance group led by two of the Men with Pointy Teeth and Bad Hair."

Ian restrained himself, not wanting to interrupt.

"Their names are . . . are . . ." Phil was fading fast.

Simian cradled his head gently. "There's a good lad. Finish the mission."

"Lestatler. And Wooldorf, I think," Phil moaned, closing his eyes. "The plan is . . ."

Everyone leaned forward.

"Come on, just a few more words," Flanders prodded.

"To keep us busy . . . fighting . . . amongst . . ."

And he expired.

Simian bowed his head, and Flanders lowered Phil gently to the ground.

"Pixie," Simian said after a moment's respectful silence, "radio our position back to Adonis please. Let them know where to send in a squad to pick up Phil's body. Nebbish, Bane, find a place to hide poor Phil until he can be retrieved."

"Aye, sir."

Ian watched in shock as they went about their sad duty. The blasted landscape and the anonymous and already-dead animals had been one thing. Watching someone pass away right in front of him was quite another.

He walked back over to the top of the hill and looked out over the expanse of the Badlands that lay ahead of them. Ian was increasingly apprehensive. He had a really bad feeling about this Creature.

\* \* \*

DESPAIR SETTLED FIRMLY over the party. Everyone kept startling and peering suspiciously at the shadows. Even Heis, if the floating eating utensils were any indication, stayed close.

"I daresay we should start keeping watches," the general said as they prepared to get some sleep. "Shifts of two hours should be about right. I'll take the first watch. Who wants to join me?"

"I will," Hutch volunteered. "Don't bobber protesting. I won't sleeb for an hour or more adyway."

"Fair enough. Off to bed for the rest of you. Get as much sleep as you can. We'll need everyone on their toes."

Soon, the camp became quiet, the gloomy night silence punctuated only by the pattering of rain on tents and Ether's gentle snoring. Ian closed his eyes but was too achy and wired to drift off. After a while, when it seemed like the rain had eased up, he gave up trying to sleep and left the tent.

He found Pixie by the fire, writing in what looked to be a journal. She smiled at his approach.

"Couldn't sleep, hey?"

"Too twitchy," Ian replied.

"I get you. It's hard to relax when on a mission."

He sat beside her. "You seem calm enough."

She shrugged, closing her journal. "This helps." She wiggled the book. "Gets the thoughts out of your head and onto paper. Experience helps too. Knowing you've been through a few things already and got through them. Listening to the calm voices, not the scared or angry ones, and especially not the ones trying to make you scared or angry. But mostly *doing* something about whatever is making you anxious. Any action is better than no action."

Ian considered that. "You're the second person to tell me something like that lately. Perhaps the universe is trying to give me a hint." After a while, he nodded in the direction of Simian, who was pacing the perimeter of the camp. "Simian's a lucky guy."

Pixie smiled. "Yes, yes, he is." She looked at him, her eyes flashing with mirth in the firelight. "We met a few years ago. I was doing freelance reconnaissance flights for residents along the Badlands border for a few years. The military asked me to serve both as a consultant and a cultural liaison for the pixies. We both ended up on a task force together, and one week after we met, he asked me out. We've been inseparable ever since."

"That's awesome," Ian said. And he meant it, even though he was the tiniest bit jealous. "I have a really stupid question about pixies."

"I'll bet it has to do with my name."

"Yes! Apparently, my question is both stupid and common."

Pixie laughed. "Our people identify each other by scent; everyone has their own unique signature. Obviously, that's really hard to translate into a written or spoken language. So here, when I said 'I'm a pixie' but couldn't provide my name, I got to be known as Pixie. We're trying to come up with a way to solve that problem, because we can't all be Pixie!"

"No, that wouldn't be very good for you," Ian said, frowning. He remembered reading how his ancestors had been forced to anglicize their Gaelic names when they immigrated and how other ethnic groups had entirely new names assigned.

"Don't worry too much," she said, patting his knee and rising to stretch. "Our friend R has a task force working on this back home, analyzing our scents for common components to see if we can get some sort of phonetic translation set up. I'm off to try to get forty beats. You should too."

Ian went back to his tent and drifted off, dreaming of blasted landscapes, phonetic translators, and long voyages to strange lands.

\* \* \*

SOMETIME LATER, Ian woke to hear Simian calling out in what he probably thought was a low voice. "How are you holding up over there?"

Simian and Hutch had posted themselves on either side of their tiny bivouac, backs to each other, keeping a lookout.

"I hab been better, but I'll lib," Hutch replied and then sneezed.

"That's the spirit, positive attitude and all that. Has Ian been helping you with research?"

"Ether started him on a running list of things we need

clarity on. We talked at length today while we marched. It might take years to sort through what he gibs us. He's very smart and knowledgeable."

Ian smiled to himself in the dark. He closed his eyes again.

"Brilliant," the gorilla said. "I do hope you'll share with the military."

"*Gnnk!*"

"What did you say?"

Silence.

"Dash it, Hutch. I hope you haven't passed out from pneumonia over there."

More silence.

Ian sat up a bit in his tent. Simian's shadow passed by as he picked his way across the campsite.

"Hutch," he said softly. "Where did you get to, old man?"

Foreboding silence.

The sound of Simian drawing his weapon.

*Rustle. Rustlerustlerustle.*

*Thump.*

"*Ooof!*"

*Whumpf.*

*Rustle.*

*Drag. Drag drag drag...*

\* \* \*

IAN SCRAMBLED out of his tent. It was still spitting rain. "Ether!" he called out. "Ether, wake up!"

The dragon groaned. "It can't possibly be morning yet. Or my shift."

"Ether, I think Simian and Hutch are gone!"

Ether's head popped out from underneath the huge tarp that served as his tent. "What?"

Within minutes, everyone had grabbed a branch from the campfire to use as a torch and was searching the area immediately surrounding their camp.

"H-h-hutch and the general are definitely gone. We should go home." Will fretted.

Pixie whistled. Everyone moved to see what she had found, their torches sputtering fitfully in the mist. She showed them a tuft of fluffy cottontail.

"They've been taken prisoner," she concluded.

The colonel clucked his tongue. "Taken right from under ouah very beaks. And noses and snouts, as the case may be."

"What do we do, Colonel?"

"Why, we pursue them o' course," he said. "Saddle up, ladies and gentlemen. Pixie, you're an excellent tracker, take point. Heis, guard her back. Give the dragon your backpacks."

Two packs floated over to Ether, who shouldered them.

"You three," the colonel pointed to the red shirts, "take up the rear. Let's move. They can't have gotten far."

They gathered everything on the double, found some proper lanterns, and started after their missing friends. They moved down the side of the hill where Phil had come up, and then they headed off the trail into the brush. Every now and then, Pixie would crouch, inspecting the ground. They kept this up for over an hour, trudging through progressively thicker and higher grass and tangles of weeds. Soon, the grass gave way to dense bracken and thorny underbrush.

Another two hours passed before Pixie crouched again, looking uncertain. "They stopped dragging Sim here," she muttered. "He's on his feet here. But . . . I can't see his footprints after that. I know he's light on his feet, but . . ."

By this time, everyone was soaked and scratched to bits. Ether's scales looked like they'd been scoured with steel wool. They waited as Pixie circled them, checking the branches, scuffing away bits of dirt with her boots. She came back to them, defeated.

"I don't understand it. I've lost them. They've just . . . vanished."

A bush suddenly leaned over and held out a branch. "Oh, for Pete's sake. You lot are so *noisy*. Is this what you're looking for?"

Pixie took a bit of cloth off the branch. "It's part of Sim's uniform! I hope he's okay."

"Guess again," the bush sniggered. It reached out and turned over the scrap of cloth. There was a dark patch of blood.

"Damn," she said softly.

Ian felt a sudden surge of chivalry, which was a bit ridiculous, as he was pretty sure Pixie was fit enough to take him down without breaking a sweat.

"Which way did they take him? And what about the rabbit?" he demanded.

"I wouldn't know," said the bush. "And if I did, I certainly wouldn't tell the likes of *you*. Now scram. This place has become a conference centre lately, and I'm tired of it. Stop bothering me."

Bone tired, worried, and soaked, Ian became thoroughly incensed. He leaned close. "You're not a fire bush, are you?"

"Of course not," the bush sniffed.

"Would you like to be?"

Pause.

"You wouldn't."

"Try me."

The bush hesitated and then laughed. "You almost had me there. It's raining, you idiot. You couldn't strike a pose in this weather, much less a match."

Ian pushed in closer. "Did I mention matches? No. Are you blind, or didn't you notice the dragon?"

"Er," the bush said.

"One breath, and you'll get a hot steam bath. Two breaths, and it will be snap, crackle, and—"

"Okay, okay!" The bush shivered all over. "They were picked up by a flying ship, and they headed east. I heard them say something about using an old theatre in the small town on the river as a staging ground for their raids. They've been running through here like rats for days."

"Who?" Ian prodded.

"Those weird dudes with bad hair and—"

"Got it." Ian nodded. "Pixie?"

Pixie already had her VRML map out. "I'm on it. Gimme a second to triangulate."

"Thanks, Mr. Bush," Ian said. "Oh, and if you've sent us on a wild goose chase . . ." He grabbed a twig and bent it backward.

"Owowowowowow!"

"Then I'll be back and it will be *pfft!*" He snapped his fingers. "You'll never see me coming. You might even call it an *ambush*."

The bush yanked its twig away and rubbed it sullenly. "Alright, alright. I get the point. Big bully."

The search party moved on, leaving the bush to sulk.

\* \* \*

THEY FOUND the town right before dawn and the theatre not long after that. It had not weathered the Badlands encroachment well. Its front windows were shattered, and a sign that read "The Globule" hung askew. The paint was blistered and peeling, and one of the front doors was off its hinges and banging in the wind.

They approached the theatre from the side, slid along the

front, and peered inside. It seemed mostly empty at the moment.

"Recommendations, Pixie?" Flanders whispered. "Mah experience is mostly on open battlefields, not this sneakin' around kind of stuff. Sim's the gorilla warrior."

"Heis stands guard here to watch for incoming. Weapons drawn, go in groups of two. Spread out through the foyer, check the box office, and make sure it's clear. Then we try the main theatre area."

Flanders nodded. "As she says. Weapons ready. At your command, Pixie."

Pixie raised a silent fist, put up two fingers, and then pointed. Two members of the group ducked inside. Heis started his invisible patrol at the front.

They made it inside without incident. No one seemed to be in the entrance area. At Pixie's direction, they gathered near one of the doors to the theatre proper. Moving quickly and quietly, they snuck inside near the back row of seats. On the stage, under a set of exceptionally bright lights, Simian and Hutch were trussed up and being questioned by what could only be henchmen: ten large teddy bears with sharp fangs, blood-red eyes, and sharp claws. Ian could see that each of them had a symbol of evil tattooed on its fuzzy belly.

"Scare bears," Ian breathed. "The stuff of toddler nightmares."

"Shh," said Pixie. "Listen."

"C'mon, General. What's it to be?" one of the bears leered. "Or not to be? Tell us all your secrets. What are a couple of rejects from Phantasmagoria doing this far into the Badlands?"

The general pressed his lips together, which, since he was a large gorilla, was an impressive sight.

The bear extended a claw and drew it slowly along Simian's cheek. "Talk, General, or this could get very painful."

Blood welled up from the scratch, but Simian didn't move.

The bear frowned. Then, apparently inspired, he picked Hutch up by the back foot. He dangled him upside down in front of Simian.

"How would you feel if I shredded your cute widdle friend here?"

Simian just smiled. "As you like it," he said and waited.

*Crunch.*

"ARGH! He bit me! Leggo! Leggo!"

It took two bears to pry Hutch off the first bear's ankle. He hobbled back to Simian. "That," he seethed, "wasn't very nice."

One of the other bears sighed. "He ain't gonna talk, Boss. Can't we just off 'im?"

Simian flinched.

Boss bear's eye's widened. "Say that again, Mugsy," he commanded, watching the general intently.

Mugsy looked bewildered. "Say what? All's I said was—"

Simian flinched again.

"Wait, wait." Boss waved the other into silence. His eyes gleamed, and he licked his lips in anticipation. "You'll have to forgive my associate," he said carefully. "He don't know nothing."

Simian blanched and gritted his teeth.

Boss bear laughed gleefully. "Well, whaddya know. Our boy's got a weakness after all!" He turned to his fellow bears. "I'll bet when he talks, he's got a stuffy accent that's veddy, veddy, proppa. Right, fellas?"

The other bears jeered, albeit uncertainly. They didn't seem sure what "veddy" might mean.

"Mugs, tell him about all your cousins."

"I only gots two, Boss."

Simian groaned.

"Keep going, Mugs."

"Ain't too much to tell, Boss," Mugs said. "Them's the ones wot got killed two years ago."

The gorilla swayed slightly but rallied and shook his head.

"I know their mom misses them alot," Mugs continued.

"NO!" Simian roared, straining against his bonds. "*Alot* is not a word! It's two words, you blithering idiot!"

At the back of the theatre, Pixie put a hand to her mouth. "We've got to do something," she said, "before they start doing terrible things to him with dangling participles."

"I say we rush them!" Will whispered, pounding a fist into his hand.

The search party turned as one to stare at him.

"What? I have my moments," he said.

"Ah think Will might be right," the colonel agreed, flexing his wingtips. "We do seem to have the element of surprise. Everyone pick a bear and charge on mah mark. Ready? Set?"

"Wait!" Pixie tried to say.

"Go!"

They all leaped up and thundered up the aisles.

"Um," Will said in their wake, "on the other hand . . ."

The party converged on stage, shouting abuse.

"For the good of the Connectome, gentlemen!"

*Blam!*

"That will teach you to speak properly!"

*Kapow!*

"I'll bet you laughed at pink dragons when you were a kid, didn't you?"

*Biff!*

"Ah, Colonel?"

Everyone stopped.

"Perhaps we should have planned this a little better," Ian said as the dust settled.

"I tried to warn you!" Pixie said.

They had all chosen the same bear. Mugsy collapsed in a heap. The other nine bears grinned evilly, because it's hard to grin any other way when you have fangs.

Boss bear held up a paw. His claws sprang out one by one. *Tictictictic ting!*

"Get 'em, boys."

The bears charged. Ian saw a flash of white on a bear leg. Seized by hope, he dived and grabbed at it, ripping away a small square of paper. He read it: DO NOT REMOVE THIS TAG.

"AIEEEEE!" the bear screamed. He toppled over, clutching his leg, and was still.

Ether swung his tail and knocked over two more bears. Flanders leaped onto Boss bear's head and started pecking madly. Another bear swung wildly at the air in front of him. Somewhere nearby, a voice said, "Nyah, nyah, missed me." The bear grunted as his stomach dented inward.

Pixie finished with one bear and lunged after another.

"Youse had better stop, or I'll kill this one!"

The melee ground to a halt as everyone stopped to see. One of the scare bears had found Will, dragged him up to the stage, and was holding a razor-sharp claw to his neck.

"I hab a bedder idea," Hutch said. Somehow, in the confusion, he'd worked himself free and grabbed Simian's gun from his holster. He was standing near the stage's edge, his back to the orchestra pit, and was pointing the gun directly at the offending bear.

The bear sneered. "You're bluffing." He drew back his paw to strike.

"Hutch!" Simian warned. "Remember that gun has a great deal of—"

BANG!

*Bipeta bipeta bipeta*

*Framp.*

*Crash.*

*Fweep.*

*Ba dum dum.*

"—recoil," Simian finished.

Kapok stuffing floated gently down.

"Jolly good shot, though."

The remaining bears surrendered hastily.

"Um, I'll just go rescue Hutch from the orchestra pit, shall I?" said Ether.

Ian untied the general, and Pixie rushed to his side.

"Simsy, are you okay?"

The gorilla turned bright red but hugged Pixie anyway. "I'm fine, dear. A little shaken. Nothing a bit of time with Strunk & White won't fix."

Pixie remembered where they were, pulled away, and bent to pick up Simian's weapon.

"All clear," came the report of the gun.

"Yes, I can see that," Simian said. Pixie gave it to him, and he patted it affectionately before holstering it. "Casualty report."

"In a moment, sah." The colonel flapped at the bears. "Step over theah, boys, and behave. Oh mah," he said, nearly tripping over a bear body. "Heis, you beat the stuffing out of this heah one. But I thought you were guarding the door."

"Certainly," Heis said. "I am."

The chicken ruffled his feathers. "I sweah entanglement gives me such a headache. Now wheah are Nebbish, Bane, and Hemlock?" Flanders pulled aside another bear body to reveal two limp human forms. "Just as ah thought." He reached down to feel for a pulse and shook his head sadly. "They're dead, Sim."

"You called, sir?" Private Hemloch, looking bruised but very much alive, struggled out from underneath a slumped-over bear.

Flanders jumped and turned to face him. "Hemlock! What are you doing?!"

"Reporting in as asked, sir. And it's Hemloch, sir."

"But ah thought for sure you'd be dead!"

"I know, sir. I'm a disgrace to this uniform. It won't happen again, sir."

"You can redeem yourself by escorting the prisoners back to headquarters for questioning," Simian said sternly.

"Of course, sir." Hemloch saluted and rounded up the bears.

Ether returned with a battered and happy rabbit.

"Did you see dat?!" he kept asking Ether while pulling a clarinet reed out of his ear. "He de one who called me cute. One shot! Bammo!"

"Yes, Hutch," Ether said, rolling his eyes at Ian. He grabbed one of the corners of the stage curtains and held it up to the rabbit's nose. "Now blow."

\* \* \*

SUDDENLY, there was the sound of slow, sarcastic clapping from above. They looked up to see two vampires sitting in the left balcony.

"Bravo," one of them drolled. "Virtuoso."

"Well, for a bunch of bit players, anyway," said the other. "Still, even with admission being free, it wasn't worth the price to get in."

"Lestatler and Wooldorf, I presume," Simian said.

"Clever monkey," replied Lestatler. "Did you train under Koko? Or Washoe?"

"Heckle all you like, pasty-face," Pixie said. "We just defeated your goon squad, and we haven't even had breakfast yet."

"What goon squad?" said Wooldorf. "I don't see anyone

we know."

"So you're saying you had nothing to do with this?"

"Nothing to do with what? All I see is a bunch of amateur actors and bad props."

Simian straightened his uniform and dusted off an epaulette. "Perhaps, my dear fellows, you can enlighten us as to why the Badlands have been expanding. Or perhaps you'd like to talk about the Creature?"

Wooldorf looked at his friend. "Expanding? What *is* he going on about?"

"No idea. The borders are the same as they've always been."

"That's not true!" Hutch said hotly. "We've seen the destruction. The damage. We were just through what used to be a beautiful landscape."

Lestatler yawned. "Oh please. It's probably part of a natural cycle. You of all people, Mr. Bunny of the fancy-shmancy elite committee, should know how little we know about this place we call home."

Wooldorf nodded. "Or maybe there's no destruction at all. Could all be a hoax."

"Liars," said Pixie.

"Call us anything you want," Lestatler said. "Just don't call us late for dinner." The pair dissolved into gales of laughter.

Simian pulled his gun, but he wasn't fast enough. Before he could level it, Wooldorf snapped his fingers, and they vanished in a puff of smoke.

"Ugh!" Will kicked a stage light in frustration. "People like that are so infuriating."

"No more so than our council," Ether said. They all looked at him. "Hutch said it. We've all seen the wasteland this area has become. It's way worse than we've been led to believe. *Way* worse. Why has the council waited so long to deal with this Creature?"

Nobody had an answer to that.

* * *

AFTER A BROKEN SLEEP in the safety of a barricaded theatre
storage room, they set out once again. As they moved out of
the little town, deeper into the Badlands, tall trees gave way
to short, gnarled ones. Smaller plants were few and far
between. The sun was low on the horizon. A sickly haze
made it difficult to see too far into the distance, and it was
unbearably hot and humid.

"AGGGH!" Ether leaped back all of a sudden, nearly
crushing Ian in the process. A pair of scorpions scattered
away from where Ether had been about to tread.

The dragon panted dramatically for a moment. "Surely
that's a sign we're getting close to our objective?"

Pixie pulled out her map. As before, a little spot marked
their location with "You are here," but this time, a big red
arrow pointed out a patch nearby marked with a skull and
crossbones. It said, "You definitely DON'T want to be here!"

"We're close," Pixie affirmed. "This is likely our objective."
She tapped the skull symbol.

Ian groaned. "I knew you'd say that."

The wind picked up, which was a small mercy. But Ian
could feel the pressure building, and he could see thunder-
heads forming behind them. They trudged along some more,
eyes down to avoid stepping on anything poisonous. The
haze thickened, and the sky began to rumble.

"W-w-we could use some light," Will said, looking
pathetic in his limp, dirty fatigues.

Lightning flashed. In the mist, Ian suddenly saw a massive
horde of emaciated people, shouting, angry, and surging
toward them. He pulled a knife and cried out in alarm.
Everyone else let out similar cries of panic and drew their

own weapons. They formed a tight circle facing outward and braced.

"What are they doing?" Ian said after a few minutes of trembling in the murk. "What are they waiting for?"

"I don't know, but I do *not* want to have to deal with a group of pissed pixies right now."

"Wait, what? Pixies? You mean dragons, right?"

"Ah saw a flock of half-dead chickens. What ah all you on about?"

"I'm not certain what I saw."

"Okay, hold up," Ian said. "Are we all seeing the same thing?"

Lightning flashed again. This time, Ian saw a deserted city, its bright neon lights dimmed or broken and its stores empty.

"I'm going to wager we all saw something different this time," the general said in a not quite steady voice.

"So," Ether nodded, "hallucinations. Nothing to worry about. Nothing at all. Ahahaha."

They stood down and began walking again. No one put away their weapons, though, and every lightning flash made them flinch. What Ian saw seemed familiar; they were the apocalyptic visions he'd seen or read somewhere: riots, wars, blasted cities, dried-up lakes, and wildfires. Seeing them brought to life was like walking through his most terrifying nightmares.

By the time Pixie held up her fist to stop, they were all wild-eyed and jittery. She motioned for everyone to get down and belly-crawl forward.

Ian scooched up beside Simian. They were at the lip of a large crater in the bedrock; the depression looked like it had been gouged out systematically in layers. It was hard to see very far into it.

An awful smell reached them, a gut-churning combination of rotting garbage, sulphur, hot metal, and exhaust fumes. The general calmly moved backward for a moment, threw up, and came back to the crater's edge.

Ether ground his teeth together. "Do we have to cross this?"

Simian shook his head. "We'll skirt the edges if we have to. I do not fancy giving the high ground to anyone who might not be a hallucination."

They pulled back from the edge and sat for a while to rest, but no one could bear to stay still for long. They moved left of the crater, keeping its lip in view but staying back far enough that whatever might be in it was unlikely to see them. They crouch-walked for another twenty minutes, glancing at the ground and surrounding area in trepidation as it slowly became devoid of anything. There were no more bodies, no animals, and no plants. It began to feel as if they were floating over nothingness. That sensation was even worse than the visions had been.

"D-do-do we have to go any further?" Will wailed.

Simian pressed his lips together firmly before answering. "I'm afraid so. We haven't completed our objective yet, and I'll be damned if I'm going to witness all this and come back empty-handed."

Hutch pricked his ears straight up and twitched. "Does anybody else hear dat?"

They listened. It sounded like a slow, primal heartbeat. The sick feeling in their stomachs was replaced by pure, cold fear.

Flanders noticed they had veered too close to the edge of the precipice and waved them down. They crept closer and peered down. Here, there was no mist, so they had a clear view. More than a thousand metres down, in the centre of the crater, was a massive dark beast in the middle of a giant black hole. With every preternatural beat, the beast convulsed, bringing black smoke, filth, and writhing, wriggling black maggots out of the hole. The sound, magnified by crater walls, was deafening.

Pixie fumbled in her backpack and pulled out a pair of binoculars. "That's got to be it," she said, trying to get them focused.

When Simian handed Ian his own binoculars, he brought the maggots into view and watched in horror as they metastasized into every element of chaos and evil he'd ever thought about: wizards, horned devils, fiery deities, jackbooted soldiers, winged demons, warlords, and gangsters. Shuddering, he moved to focus on the beast at the centre.

"Oh no," he breathed and went very still.

"Steady on," Simian said, as much to Ian as everyone else. "Let's not lose our nerve now. Gear up. Let's get what information we can."

Everyone pulled out the devices they'd gotten from R and began collecting data. Simian tried focusing a bizarre-looking camera. "Drat," he said. "Not close enough."

"I'll go in, General," Hutch volunteered.

"Admirable, but no," Simian said. "I daresay they'd see you coming for ages before you could get close enough, and you'd be so much rabbit stew. No. Going on foot is not the answer."

Ether sighed and stuck out his claw for the camera. "Subtlety is not a hallmark of your command, General."

"Ether, you can't! You'll get swatted out of the sky!" Will protested.

"Nonsense," Ether said, laying a finger across his nose. "There are *some* advantages to being me."

He lunged into the air and flew toward the centre of the crater. As they watched, he shrank until he was barely large enough to handle the weight of the camera. Then he disappeared from view altogether.

They waited for what seemed like forever, measuring, observing, and worrying. The slow pulsing echoed in their ears and reverberated in their bones. The coldness in their stomachs settled into leaden weights. Ian wondered how they'd ever feel normal again.

Finally, Ether returned, looking battered and bruised. The camera lens was smashed, and the strap was in tatters, barely hanging on.

"Mission accomplished, General," he croaked. Ian cursed and rushed to prop him up.

"E-ether, what happened?" Will asked.

"Got too close," he said, breathing hard. "General, we've got to get this information to the council as soon as possible. We've got a huge fight on our hands."

"Agreed." the general nodded. "Fall back!"

* * *

BY THE TIME they made it back to the edge of the Complexus, they all looked like Ether. Flanders had lost half his back feathers in a battle with a rabid dog. Hutch limped badly and shivered constantly as they'd also encountered several bands of the darklings released by the Creature. Will was one large bruise, Pixie and Simian had several cuts and scrapes each, and Ian sported a long, painful gash down his leg.

They dragged themselves to the Centre for Engine Nearing. R greeted them.

"General, we've been expecting you," he said.

"Glad to hear it, R," the general replied. "We have some information which we'll gladly exchange for medical attention, a hot bath, and a soft bed."

R smiled at them. "Deal. Come this way," he said, tottering off in the direction of the residence.

* * *

THE NEXT MORNING, everyone seemed to be in better health and humour. Hutch looked pleased with his bandages, in part because they made him look heroic. After enjoying a big breakfast provided by the Centre, they ventured into the laboratory complex. The general's clearance gave them access to the top-secret research area, where they found R hunched over a desk, muttering to himself. He didn't notice their approach until Simian cleared his throat noisily.

"Ah!" R jumped. "Good morning, everyone. Feeling better?"

Ether smiled. "Much better. Your staff is great."

Ian smirked. "He's only saying that because they served fresh peaches for breakfast."

R grinned. "They're my favourite too." The smile quickly disappeared from his face. "I'm afraid, though, that's the best news you're going to get all day."

"Ah take it you have had some time to check ovah the data we collected?"

R nodded. "I've been at it all night." He gestured that they should crowd around his desk. It was covered with photos. R picked up a handful of papers. "As you know, our initial intelligence reports on the Creature were inconclusive." As he waved the papers, Ian could see that most of them were marked with single words like "big" and "scary." He was beginning to suspect that Hagar had a point about the council's scouts.

"And even some of your information has been less than useful." R indicated half a dozen pictures that had been pushed aside. The view in each of them was obscured by a big pink dragon thumb.

"You try flying low over a vicious antagonist surrounded

by henchmen and see how many happy hallmarked moments *you* get!" Ether sniffed.

"Sorry?" R looked puzzled.

"A reference from the Other Side," Ian said. "Sort of. I'll explain later."

"I see." R shook his head to clear it, making his hair stick straight up. "Well, as I was about to say, the remaining data, including the other photographs, were extremely helpful. But the information itself isn't encouraging and, in many cases, leads to more questions."

"In what way?" Pixie asked.

"Well," R sighed, "the Creature will be a tough opponent. It's got an exoskeleton that will act like virtually indestructible armour. It has compound eyes, which means it can detect movement from almost any direction and react to it. It has powerful wings and legs, so it can walk, fly, or jump very quickly and cover huge distances."

"And those are just its defences," Ian muttered.

"Exactly," R agreed. "We're not sure if it has any offensive capabilities, other than producing all those darklings you observed."

The general's face was like thunder. "Any suggestions on how to beat it?"

R looked glum. "Nothing yet, but we're working on it."

"What about the hole?" Pixie asked.

"That's the other problem," R replied. "It appears to be a rift between our plane of existence and another, much like what you proposed in your dissertation years ago, Ether."

"You proposed rifts?" Ian was startled. "I thought Merlin did that."

Ether shrugged modestly. "What Merlin did was discover how to *make* small rifts to allow us to observe and possibly travel to the Other Side. But the theory about there being an Other

Side to begin with, and that the Flux flows from there through a Great Rift to here, well that was me. I spent a *very* long time observing how the Flux works and what came out of it. The data was so confusing. I had to rewrite several chapters a number of times. And getting time with my supervisor was impossible!"

"I'm impressed," Ian said.

Ether blinked back tears. "Thanks, Ian. That means a lot to me." He fumbled for a handkerchief. "Sorry. I'm being too emotional. I still get flashbacks."

"Flashbacks?"

"PDTS. Post-doctoral traumatic stress disorder."

"The hole?" Pixie prompted.

"Ah yes." R focused again. "Well, if that's the case, then this likely is another rift like you discussed, Ether. But as to why it's located in the Badlands, or why it seems so predominantly negative, well, I have to say we told you so."

"Eh?" said Ether.

"We filed reports every year warning the council to monitor things more closely in the Badlands and to start mitigating the spread of it before it got too big."

Simian and Pixie glanced at each other, clearly not pleased to learn this.

One of the guards posted outside the laboratory opened the door. "General, sir, there's a Private Hemloch out here to see you. Says he has urgent information."

"Send him in."

Hemloch came in and saluted smartly. "I have some new details on the Badlanders for you, sir."

"Come, come. Let's have it."

"While you were away, sir, I took the liberty of questioning the bears we took into custody. I thought time was of the essence, sir, which is why I didn't wait for your orders."

"Time *is* of the essence, Hemlock. Get on with it, man."

"Hemloch, sir. Yes, sir. The bear confessed that his boss

had received orders from Lestatler to gather all bears at the edge of the Badlands, at the closest entry point to the council chambers. He seemed to think other creatures were massing along the borders too."

"By God!" Simian smashed a huge ape fist into the desk, making R jump. "That sounds like a plan of attack if I ever heard one! Did you get anything else, Hemloch?"

"No, sir. He was mostly incoherent. He kept repeating 'rabbit go bang!' the whole time."

Hutch sniffled happily.

"If ah may suggest, General, I do believe it is time for battle stations."

"Agreed. Send a messenger to the council with a summary of our data and a request for high alert status Collectome-wide. I'm certain the Creature will waste no time connecting our bear engagement with the sudden appearance of a camera-happy dragon near the Great Rift. They may accelerate whatever plans they have. Pixie, summon the Jabberwalk."

"Yes, sir," she said and ran out.

"Colonel, you're with me. We need to draw up plans fast," Simian said and headed for the door.

"W-w-what about us?" asked Will.

"Er," the general stopped midstride. "Help R with whatever you can further interpret from the reconnaissance mission. When you're done here, get some rest. You especially, Ian, you're looking rather pale. We'll set up a makeshift headquarters in one of the nearby buildings. Report there to find out where we're going to establish a front. And be at the command post at dawn."

\* \* \*

EARLY THE NEXT MORNING, Ian woke with a start to find Ether peering down at him. The dragon's face seemed huge; his eyes twinkled mischievously.

"I was going to see if you had ticklish feet, but you woke up before I had a chance to test you."

Ian groaned and looked around groggily. He had been sleeping on a makeshift cot; he seemed to be sheltered by a large swath of cloth with a dog motif.

"Right," he said, remembering. "The pup tent."

"So far, so good." Ether grinned. "C'mon, it's nearly dawn."

Ian fumbled for his clothes and staggered out of the tent. He blinked in surprise. It seemed that the general had been very busy overnight.

The place teemed with soldiers of all shapes and statures. There were red shirts and mages with long flowing robes, women wearing tight black leather and dark glasses, and several large animals, including lions, tigers, and bears.

"Oh my," said Ether. "Check it out."

Ian looked and frowned. The carnival-like atmosphere was not helped by the presence of Honest Ed da Mouse.

"Bets please!" he shouted. "Place your bets here! Odds on all major battles and characters. Bets please!"

Ian exhaled noisily and shook off his remaining sleepiness. "Let's go find the general."

They found him at a large desk inside the command post, surrounded by maps and various platoon leaders. He barked out a set of orders and then turned his attention to Ether and Ian.

"Good lads," he said, beaming at their punctuality. The smile faded quickly. "Our worst fears have come true. There are Badlander troops on the border, and the Creature himself is expected to arrive on the front by midday. It is war after all, gentlemen."

Ether nodded gravely. "The council's orders?"

"They're not convinced we need to do anything!" Simian clamped down on his frustration. "We're to attempt peace talks, if you can believe it. They want the Origins Committee to act as envoy. I've already sent a request to Lestatler for a parley."

Ether rolled his eyes. "Why doesn't the council send someone official? We're academics!"

The general shrugged. "Council didn't say, except that their main concern was keeping order in the rest of the Connectome. They wished to remain at the chambers to . . ." the general paused to pick up and read a note, "'indicate to the citizenry that there is no need for panic and that their council is in control of the situation.'"

"There wouldn't happen to be an emergency bunker at these chambers, would there?" Ian asked. "Someplace to go in case of danger?"

Ether snorted. "Why, Ian, how shockingly cynical of you."

"He's not incorrect," Simian said. "They have all retreated to safer positions within Bureaucracy Prime. Should peace talks fail, however, the council has only said that they want us to study the matter further. Not enough data."

"Study it!" Ether grumped. "I studied it up close. I can tell you we're in big trouble if we don't act now."

The general nodded. "Agreed. That's why I've gone ahead and set up a defence line. They didn't say I *couldn't* . . ."

Pixie came into the command post. "We're ready, General."

They followed Pixie outside, where the rest of the Origins Committee was already waiting by the Jabberwalk, yawning sleepily in the half-light.

R came running up to the general. "Sir," he said. "I need some voice of authority here. The Eunuchs Corps are in an argument, and I can't get them to stop. I've never seen them act this way before. They're holding up assembly of the Anti-Creature Machine."

In the distance, Ian could see two hefty-looking, pasty-faced guys shouting at each other.

"Chrnod 775!" one yelled.

"No! Chmod 772!" the other yelled back.

"Mget lost!" the first said rudely.

"Finger!" said the other even more rudely and with a quick gesture.

The general slapped a hand to his face and rubbed it in frustration. "Go on to try peace talks without me, but report back as soon as you return. And watch your step out there." He addressed them all, but his gaze lingered on Pixie. He stomped off in the direction of the eunuchs, while the Origins Committee clambered into the Jabberwalk.

\* \* \*

By the time the ship limped back to Phantasmagoria two hours later, General Simian had worn a spot in the command post floor with his pacing. He rushed outside to greet them, and Ian could see him counting heads as they disembarked.

"Well?" Simian said, huffing with impatience.

"Lestatler opened the talks by demanding complete and total subservience of the Connectome." Ether sighed.

The general bristled at the thought. "And you said?"

Ether grinned. "Nuts to that. We countered by saying we'd agree not to pound them into the turf if they all ran back home."

The general took off his beret and polished the badge on the front of it. "Jolly good," he said with satisfaction. "And what was his reply to that?"

Ether appeared to consider this. "I believe his exact words were 'Smite me.'"

Simian snorted. "Well, that settles it. But what took you so long? If that's truly all that was said, you should have been back ages ago."

Pixie smiled wanly. "The border area is now completely unstable. With the Badlanders pushing forward, there's a great deal of turmoil. Enough to make escape very difficult."

"Pixie is being too modest," Ian said. "It was terrible, not only because of the storms but we were being shot at. It's only because of her good driving skills that we made it out."

"General," Ether said, worry all over his face, "the first wave of Badlanders wasn't far behind us. And if you add the new area to previous estimates, the territory might be up as high as forty percent."

"No time to waste." He spun around. "Colonel!"

"Yes, sah?"

"It's time to engage the enemy!"

"Sah!"

* * *

LESS THAN HALF AN HOUR LATER, the first of the Badlanders appeared on the horizon. From his vantage point overlooking the battlefield, Ian could see that it was a lone figure dressed in black.

He wore a dark mask and hood; only his eyes remained visible. He carried a long, thin sword on his back. He walked stealthily to the centre of the field, assumed a fighting stance, and called out a challenge.

"Hiiiiiiii yah!"

The general nodded grimly. "An e5. Exactly what I would have started with. We'll have to counter with e4." He stood up from his chair, tugged his tunic down sharply, and gave his first order. "Engage."

Flanders turned around and clucked loudly at a platoon

commander. He in turn yelled at a group of soldiers dressed in white gis, one of whom trotted out to the Badlander to face him. The others followed close behind.

For a moment, nobody moved. Then Ian could see one of the soldiers' mouths move. A few seconds later, a voice said, "You killed my father, and now you must die!"

The black warrior sniffed haughtily. "If you can take this sword from my hands, you might be worthy of the ground my father spat upon." His mouth continued working for several seconds after his voice had faded from hearing.

The first white-clad soldier suddenly jumped forward and attacked. Their fists connected with the sound of two bamboo sticks coming together. The other white-gi'd soldiers formed a ring around the fight.

Within minutes, the black warrior had dispatched the first assailant, and a second had leaped in front of him. The others patiently waited their turn.

Hutch looked disgusted. "Dis is ridiculous! Why don't dey all attack at once?"

Ether flipped through a box of Origin files he'd had delivered to command. "Says here that's the way it's supposed to wor—"

"Oh for Pebe's sake!" Hutch said. "Dis is gonna take all day." He jumped off his seat and ran onto the field.

"Hutch! Wait!" Ether called.

Too late.

Hutch hopped over to the rapidly dwindling ring of white soldiers and waited. Another Phantasmagoria representative jumped into the fray. He tried to kick the black warrior but was blocked.

"Ha!"

"Hee!

"Heeya!"

"Ha! Ho!"

There was a streak of brown fur at the Badlander's ankle.

"Ha! OW!!!" The Badlander grabbed at his leg and hopped up and down.

*Zip. Crunch.*

"OW! OW!" The Badlander grabbed his other ankle, hovered for the exact amount of time it took him to realize he had nothing to support him, and crashed to the ground. He struggled to sit up.

Hutch leaped up, leg and forepaw extended, ears forward. Time stalled as he delivered a beautiful four-part spinning-leg-ear kick in slow motion.

*Slap. Slap. Slap. Slap.*
"Choo!"

The Badlander collapsed in a heap. A cheer went up on the Phantasmagoria side.

Hutch jogged back to the post, picking tabi from his front teeth.

"Well done, old man!" The general slapped him on the back, sending him sprawling. "I had quite forgotten your black belt in carroté."

"Danks, General."

"Colonel!"

"Yes, sah!"

By now, more Badlanders had gathered in the field. They watched uneasily as Flanders' troops wheeled several large crates forward. Flanders raised a wing, and the troops picked up large crowbars, setting them against the crate seams. With a decisive movement, the colonel brought his wing down, and one by one, the crate lids popped off.

Suddenly, the air was filled with hundreds of cooing grey pigeons wearing miniature leather flight caps, goggles, and tiny white scarves. They all clutched tiny black balls in their feet.

As Ian watched, they circled once to get into formation

and then flew out toward the enemy. He strained to see. "What on earth?" he asked.

"Standard-issue Skinner Pigeon powder bombs," Simian said. "Observe."

The pigeons swooped toward the Badlanders. As soon as they were close enough, the first pigeons began dropping the little black balls, which exploded on contact. Some of the first wave of Badlanders broke and ran as bear bits flew everywhere.

"Ewww." Ether curled his lip as a set of fangs landed at his feet.

"Let's hope it's enough," Simian said and then bellowed, "DM! Where's the DM?!"

A young woman in a long brown robe came up to the post. "Yes, General?" she intoned.

"Damage?"

The DM reached into her robe and pulled out several multi-sided dice. She rolled them in her hands a few times and then let them spill onto the ground. She crouched to inspect them.

"Six points to the ninjas, four points to the bears, and two to the kobolds," she reported.

"Damn," the general said.

"Still, sah, it is a good first strike," Flanders admonished.

"It's not nearly enough," Simian said.

\* \* \*

HEMLOCH JOGGED UP. "EXCUSE ME, SIRS."

Flanders clucked. "Ah am beginning to dislike the sight o' you, son. Ah hope it's good news you ah bringing."

"No, sir," Hemloch panted. "I've just returned from the chambers to tell you that a surprise party of evil dwarfs has sacked the Academy of Writing Analysis."

"Oh doh!" Hutch cried.

"What's that?" Ian asked Ether.

"In some of our glimpses through the rifts, we've been able to take pictures of human writing," Ether replied. "You know, books, letters, reports. Especially notes made for projects. The academy was set up recently to analyze the stuff for clues about our origins and basic human thought patterns. We thought if we got a handle on how you guys thought, we might predict what could show up in the Connectome. It was all very experimental and hypothetical."

"Wow, that's pretty ambitious," Ian said.

Ether nodded agreement. "It was Hutch's idea."

"There's not much left of the place, I'm afraid. They may have used magical thinking to wish for its destruction," Hemloch was saying as he handed over a few sheets of completely unintelligible characters.

Hutch moaned. "I can't read these anymore. The whole place must be in runes."

Ian winced.

Flanders ruffled his feathers. "Dispatch guards to all other major centres of study, and pass the word to the commandah at Complexus to do the same. It is apparent the Badlanders are waging an anti-factual campaign."

Simian meanwhile had turned his attention to the battle-field. The Badlanders had sent six female darkling mages forward. They wore deep purple robes and had frizzy green hair. They intoned an incantation, turned themselves into big purple rhinoceroses, charged into the Skinner crates, and smashed them to pieces.

"Tell Merlin to do his thing," Simian muttered.

In a few minutes, there was a flash of light, and half a dozen blue squirrels darted out to bite the rhinoceroses' toes. In the confusion, the rhinos ran into each other and crashed to the ground.

As more Badlanders appeared, Simian sent his troops out to meet them. Soon, the whole battlefield was covered with soldiers of all shapes and sizes. Claws, hooks, beaks, hooves, and hands grappled and fought.

The members of the Origins Committee helped where they could. Ether took to the sky to rain ice glitter down on a group of fire demons. Ian took out several squadrons of bears with his now-patented rip-and-trip move. Will hid behind a tree and pelted advancing troops with rocks. The progress of Heis and Hutch could be monitored, determined by whether Badlanders clutched their stomachs or gripped their ankles.

The day extended into evening, but the Badlanders still kept coming. Then, the news that no one had wanted to hear finally arrived.

The Creature was coming.

\* \* \*

SIMIAN BEGAN to call for a fallback.

"Ready the ACM!" Flanders bellowed.

They could hear the slow heartbeat again, growing louder as the Creature approached. The sound made Ian run back to the command post even faster.

When he turned, he could see the Creature roiling over the land toward them. Incredibly, the hole had come with him, pulsing out dark, smoky air that soon spread out across the battlefield like a fog of war.

With a tremendous boom, Pixie smashed through the doors of a makeshift hangar and drove the Anti-Creature Machine to the edge of the battlefield. It was a huge machine —a tangled mass of pulleys and levers, ropes and wires, and tubes and pipes. Pixie threw the device into park and ran around the back. She pulled a large ball bearing from her ammo pouch and held it over a funnel. She looked at the general.

"Fire at will," he said.

"NOOOOOO!" Will screamed and dived behind a crate that hadn't been smashed.

Flanders moved to reassure him. "Theah, theah," he said, peering through the leaves. "Ah am sure the general didn't mean you." Pixie dropped the bearing into the funnel.

It rolled around the rim for a second, rattled down the pipe, and dropped onto a slanted board. From there, it fell off and hit a lever, which swung sideways and released a tiny windmill.

The windmill pivoted on its axis until it caught the breeze and started spinning. At the other end of the windmill, a small electromagnet spun, surged, and sent a tiny bolt of electricity crackling along a wire. The bolt sizzled along for about a metre and moved onto a metal plate where a hamster in a cage labelled "Rube" sat peacefully chewing a sunflower seed.

*Fizzot!*

"YAHOOIEE!" the hamster screeched and jumped, whapping his head on a big red button.

Everyone held their breath.

The ACM shuddered once, twice, and then catapulted a large white blob into the air. The blob arced slowly over the battlefield, soaring higher and higher until it reached its apex and began its descent. As its shadow passed overhead, the fighting ground to a halt as soldiers stopped to watch . . . as . . . . it . . . came . . . down . . .

*Sploch.*

The Creature rocked backward with the impact of the heavy wet goo. The Creature flailed and tried to surge forward, but the goo got stiffer and harder the more it struggled.

"Direct hit!" Pixie shouted.

A cheer went up while the hamster swore and stubbed out its tail.

"What is it?" Ian asked.

"Ooblek," Ether said. "Wicked stuff."

Suddenly, the Creature went limp, and the goo covering its body liquefied and slid off it.

"Uh-oh," Will offered.

The beast reared up and came crashing down, opening its mouth to roar. The sound was long and loud and low, and it made the ground shake violently. Black smoke poured out of its mouth.

Pixie cursed and reached into her pouch to draw out two fistfuls of bearings. The hamster saw this, squeaked in horror, and jumped up to pound the red button frantically.

Several more blobs streaked across the sky. The first two missed the Creature but flattened a group of demon spawn nearby. The next eight were direct hits, halting the beast's forward motion. Again the beast relaxed, waiting until the goo dribbled away. Then it reached out with a long arm and swept aside an entire platoon of red shirts.

Then it screamed again.

This time the wave was more force than noise, and it cut a swath right up through the centre of the battlefield, ripping up turf and sending bodies flying in all directions.

"That's heading for us!" Ether yelled. He grabbed as many people as he could and heaved himself into the air. The wave rumbled underneath them and blew the command post into a thousand pieces.

The edge of the wave caught Ether and threw him backward onto the ground.

"We're in trouble," he groaned.

Simian struggled out from underneath Ether's wing. "Retreat and regroup at the designated coordinates!" he shouted. "Pixie! Keep firing that thing, but target other enemies!"

"Yes, sir!" she replied and jumped into the ACM to reposition it.

From across the field, they could hear a deep, guttural laugh that chilled their very souls. The Creature was still advancing.

The fighting continued until it was too dark for even the Badlanders to see. Phantasm soldiers dragged themselves back from the front and made uneasy camp in the inky blackness. A chill wind blew in from the Badlands, and thunderclouds gathered in the distance. The members of the Origins Committee helped set up a new makeshift command post at their second fallback position and listened glumly as Simian and Flanders took in casualty reports.

". . . and most of the mages are severely drained," Hemloch said. "Although we did do well against the Dracknor Dragons."

Ether, lying upside down with all four feet in the air, smiled faintly.

But Simian waved it aside. "All very well, dammit, but we lost a lot of ground today. Another day like this and we'll be past the point of no return."

Ian, who had been staring into the campfire, looked up sharply at this. "What do you mean?"

"If we can't hold them off with a majority advantage, we certainly won't be able to with less than that." He got up and started pacing again. "That Creature is far smarter than I gave him credit for, and he's obviously well-versed in the art of war. I've never seen the Badlanders this organized. We simply *must* take him out."

Ian rubbed his hands up and down his thighs, looking agitated. "We may not be able to," he said finally.

Simian stopped drumming his fingers and seemed to sit

up higher. "You're right, Ian. With this kind of attitude I'm projecting, we won't. I cannot let one bad day on the field bring me down, and I certainly can't let my troops see me in this state." He nodded sharply. "Thank you for reminding me of this."

He made a visible effort to pull himself together and then got up to go talk to his troops. They could hear him talking to his soldiers in a hearty voice, projecting confidence and hoisting morale up by its undershorts, if need be.

At the campfire, Ether rolled over and looked suspiciously at Ian. "That's not what you meant at all, is it?" he asked Ian.

Ian just looked miserable.

Ether jumped up, grabbed Ian by the arm, and dragged him out of earshot.

"You know something about the Creature that you haven't told us, don't you?" Ether said. "There's something you're not saying."

Ian tried to shake his head but stopped. He couldn't look Ether in the eyes.

"You haven't said much since we saw him," Ether persisted, "and you go all white and funny-looking every time we talk about him. Ian, what aren't you telling me?"

Still no answer.

"Ian! Lives are at stake here!"

Ian groaned and sat down abruptly, burying his face in his hands. Finally, he said, "His name isn't Creature."

Ether sat directly in front of Ian and propped his claws on his knees. "And?"

Ian dropped his hands. "His name is Cotwo, not Creature. You've got it wrong."

"So? What difference does his name make? And how do you know this?"

Ian swallowed hard. "Because I-I created him."

There was a long, stunned silence.

"Ian," Ether said quietly. "Ian. Tell me you didn't say that."

Ian rubbed a hand over the back of his neck. "Cotwo was the ultimate enemy in my game," he said. "The boss. You must have seen my shelf."

"Of course I did," Ether said, growing angry. "But I didn't look at it closely. What in the name of the Connectome made you write something as horrible as that?!"

"Grimdark was popular," Ian said, getting defensive. "Major characters were being killed off in all the game franchises. Dystopias were all the rage on television and in the movies. All the awards were going to post-apocalyptic books! I wanted my work to be taken seriously!"

Ether threw up his hands. "Great, Ian! That's just great!" he stormed. "Depressing sells. Great justification."

"It was more than that," Ian said hotly. "It was an exploration of the darker side of human nature. Cotwo was a metaphor for the big, unsolvable problems of our era."

"Oh, brilliant!" Ether said sarcastically. "Like we need further evidence of man's inhumanity!" He reached out and smacked Ian on the head. "Hello? Earth to Ian?! Read a history book if you want darkness and brutality. Read your newspapers and magazines. You don't need to keep *exploring* it in stories, for cryin' out loud!" Ether got up and stomped around in a circle. "I swear I will never understand the human penchant for looking under rocks to examine dark, ugly things."

Now Ian stood up. "Well, we can't pretend humans aren't evil! And we can't pretend we haven't royally screwed things up!"

"Of course not," Ether raged. "But you don't have to keep fostering the idea either! Did it ever occur to you that by constantly announcing that humanity has a bad side that you're helping to perpetuate it? Develop it, even?"

"That's ridiculous."

"*Blast it*, Ian!" Ether thundered. "Human beings are among some of the most complex and wonderful creatures ever made. But just like any complex system, they're extremely unstable. The tiniest little thing can set them off. Heaven only knows what prolonged exposure can do to such a system!"

"But I can't be held responsible for how my work is interpreted!" Ian tried one more time.

"No," Ether agreed. "Because if it's another thing you lot are good at, it's getting six different meanings from the same five words. But you *are* ultimately responsible for choosing what sort of emotions and thoughts you *set out* to invoke in people. I don't suppose this book of yours had any redeeming qualities, like say, a happy ending? Mankind overcoming evil—that sort of thing?"

Ian's shoulders slumped in defeat. "No," he mumbled. "He's meant to be indestructible. Every character dies in the end, and the planet is left a wasteland."

"Wonderful." Ether shook his head. "So your message in the game was don't bother, give up, we can't win, and humanity was a waste of time."

Ian opened his mouth to protest and closed it again. "I guess it was."

Ether lunged forward and picked Ian up bodily. He leaped into the air and started flying.

"Ether! What are you doing?"

The dragon's wings thrashed the air. "It's time to write a sequel."

* * *

As Ether climbed higher and higher, Ian started to get nervous.

"Where are you taking me?" he asked, not daring to look down.

Ether didn't answer but instead strained upward even harder. After a few more minutes of this, he stopped to hover. He gestured wildly with his tail. There was a loud popping noise, followed by a long, low hissing sound. A bright circle of light appeared in front of them.

Ether ducked through it, and suddenly, they were above a sprawling city. Ether twisted until he was able to grab his notepad and pencil from underneath one of his scales.

"Here," he said firmly, handing them to Ian. "Start writing."

"What?! Here?!" Ian squirmed so he could see where they were. "Up here?"

"Yep." Ether grinned evilly.

"But, Ether, I haven't been able to write anything for ages! You know that! What am I supposed to write?"

"A sequel—with a happy ending."

"But I have writer's block, Ether. I haven't written a word in months!"

"That's because you've been trying to write the wrong stuff, and all you need is a little inspiration." With that, he switched his grip to Ian's ankles, letting him drop and dangle.

"AGGGGGHHHHHHHHHEAREYOUOUTOFYOUR- MIND—OW!" Ian winced as his head bumped into something. He strained his neck to see. It was the top of a very tall building.

"AGGGGGHHHH! ETHER, THIS IS THE CN TOWER! ONE OF THE TALLEST BUILDINGS IN THE WORLD! DO YOU HAVE ANY IDEA HOW HIGH UP WE ARE??!!'"

"Hmm," Ether pondered. "Well, if that tourist book I read at your house is anything to go by, about . . . 553 metres."

"ETHERRRR!!!!"

The dragon let his arms quiver for a moment. "Oh goodness me! My arms are getting soooo tired. Perhaps I'll rest one." He let go of one ankle.

"AGGGGGHHHH!"

"Your vocabulary is getting awfully limited again, Ian. Not a good start to a sequel."

"Alright, alright!!" Ian closed his eyes and tried to ignore the pounding noises his heart was making. After he composed himself, he opened his eyes and scratched madly on the notepad.

"There," he said after several terrifying minutes. "It's done."

"See?" Ether said. "S'mazing what you can accomplish with a little focus."

"Now what?" Ian muttered.

"Now we have to find a place to distribute your master-work so people read it. We need a fairly large group. Any suggestions?"

Ian tried to quell the swimming sensation that had spread from his head to his toes.

"We're close to a stadium here, I think."

Ether squinted down at the cityscape. "Well, well," he said with satisfaction. "You mean that tiny, itty, bitty circle waaaay down there on the ground is actually a big ball park but doesn't look that way because we're so . . . high up?"

"Ether," Ian said through gritted teeth, "did anyone ever tell you that you have a sadistic sense of humour?"

The dragon twisted again so that he was dangling face to face with Ian. "Not until recently, no," he said and plunged into a nosedive.

"Etheeeeeerrrrrr!"

The dragon pulled up about three hundred feet above the stadium. There was a game in progress, and the place was packed. "Hold the notepad out in front of you, Ian."

"Can they see us?"

Ether had closed his eyes and was concentrating hard. "Not while my magic holds. I hope nobody notices how weird the shadow on the field looks."

Ian looked down to see a distinctly dragon-shaped silhouette on the playing field.

"The notepad, Ian. Quickly now."

Still upside down, Ian held the notepad out in front of him. The pages with his notes flew off and fluttered away into the crowds.

"Ether! We've lost them!"

"Keep looking."

Ian watched in amazement as a second copy of his notes appeared on the pad and flew away. A third and fourth copy followed, and soon the pad was gushing bits of paper.

"Great," Ian muttered. "I'm being held prisoner by a flying photocopier."

Ether loosened his grip on Ian's ankle ever so slightly.

"AGGGGGHHHH! Ether! Cut that out!"

"How are we doing?"

Ian checked out the crowds and saw that people were picking up the papers and reading them. "I think it's working."

"Good," Ether said. "A few more minutes here, and then we'll buzz the downtown core for good measure."

Ian groaned.

* * *

THEY WERE PERCHED atop one of the city's many condo buildings, Ian fighting dizziness from the super-speedy flyover they had completed. "N-now what?"

"Not sure. I have no idea how many human minds need to be aware of something for it to show up in the Connectome. How else can we reach a lot of people quickly?"

Ian thought for a minute, desperate to avoid another flight. "Internet?"

"Perfect! Where can we access it?"

Ian patted his pockets for his phone, but it was nowhere to be found. He closed his eyes. His whole life had been on that thing.

"Well?" Ether demanded.

"Internet café? If those are still a thing?"

"Right. Off you go to find one. Meet me back here in a couple of hours."

"What?! How am I supposed to get down?"

"Oh." Ether scratched his chest. "Of course." He looked around and spotted a roof access door. Trundling over, they found that it was locked.

"Now what?"

"Piece of cake," Ether replied. "Stand back." Ether bent over, formed his mouth into a near perfect O, and blew a precise, concentrated stream of freezing glitter at the lock. It crackled as it froze solid. He turned around, aimed a careful kick with a powerful back leg, and the entire door ripped right off its hinges.

The lock finished shattering a moment later.

"Oops."

"I'll say."

"Well, got the job done, anyway," Ether said. "Down you go. It's probably only thirty floors."

"How am I going to explain being in the service stairwell if I get caught?"

Ether hunted under his scales and found a squeegee, which he gave to Ian. "Congratulations. You're a window cleaner."

"Why . . .?"

"Great for cleaning scales," Ether explained. "Now, shoo."

Ian began the long trip down, holding the squeegee in

front of him like some sort of warding talisman. At ground level, after forty-five minutes of searching and accosting several random strangers who looked like they might know the neighbourhood, he found an Internet café on Yonge St. Mercifully, it was offering free Internet with the purchase of a coffee today, and he still had a few coins in his pocket that he had been carrying since he'd landed in the Connectome. He collapsed into a seat, his knees and feet burning with use, and sipped the hot brew gratefully.

He sat there, bouncing his knee nervously, wondering what to do. He got a few quizzical glances as he sat there, and he wondered why until he realized how he was dressed. "Uh, testing the cosplay for the next Comiccon," he said to the guy at the next table, who gave him a sarcastic thumbs-up.

Ian sighed, turned to his screen, and started typing random ideas into the search bar. Set up a blog? Would take too long and wouldn't have visitors. Social media? He didn't have enough followers to make it worthwhile, and they'd probably wonder why the heck he was suddenly posting the tail end of a story on his feed. What to do, what to do?

*Aha.* Storytelling apps. He clicked on the first result, set up an account under a pen name, and started typing so furiously that the guy at the text table decided to put some distance between them.

* * *

SOMETIME LATER, Ian hauled himself through the service door, gasping. "Stairs," he groaned and laid down to catch his breath. But Ether wasn't having any of it. He grabbed Ian and launched them both bodily off the building, creating a portal to drop into on the way down.

When Ian and Ether arrived back in the Connectome, they appeared right over the top of Cotwo. The Creature immediately sensed their presence, drew back an arm, and bashed them out of the sky. Ether screamed, and they went hurtling toward their camp, crash-landing on the ACM, which collapsed with a bang.

The shouts of alarm that had gone up quickly changed to calls for a medic and dismayed yelps as flashlights were turned on the remains of the ACM. Hands appeared out of the darkness to pull Ian out of the wreckage.

Simian strode up moments later, followed by the rest of the committee. "What's all this ruckus?" he demanded. He stopped, clearly shocked by the sight of the destroyed ACM.

Ether whimpered as he was pulled free. "My wing . . . Careful please. It hurts really bad."

"Ether?" Simian said. "What the devil?"

"So sorry, General," Ether said, wheezing in pain as someone touched him. "That thing has wicked good luck."

"Explain."

"We reappeared over the Creature. Cotwo. He smashed us into the ACM."

"Reappeared? Where have you been?" Pixie asked.

Ian struggled to sit up, biting back his own grunts of agony. He could barely move his ankle, and there were what must have been dozens of splinters—or worse—jammed into his back. As the flashlight beams moved over Ether, he was horrified to see that a wing was clearly broken in at least two places.

"We went to the Other Side. I tried to get Ian to write a sequel."

"A sequel?" Hutch rubbed his nose. "From the beginning, dragon, you're not making any sense."

Ether would only glare at Ian.

"The Creature," Ian finally said wretchedly. "I made it. For my game."

Everyone within hearing range gasped.

"I didn't mean for it to be here. I didn't know! I had no idea." Ian wrung his hands. "It's the boss monster. In the game, it's indestructible. Ether took me back to write a sequel to the game. To get rid of it. I . . . I don't think it worked."

"Not enough people read it?" Pixie asked.

Ian shrugged. "I don't know. Maybe."

"Or it wasn't believable enough!" Ether spat. "What exactly did you write?"

"Perhaps we need to give what I wrote time enough to get here from the Flux?" Ian said desperately.

"What *did* you write, Ian?" Flanders clucked.

"Aliens," Ian muttered. "I said that aliens arrived at the last minute, blasted it to pieces, and then went on to open a trade agreement to help Earth rebuild."

"Aw jeez." Will sat down heavily. "He resorted to a deus ex machina. Nobody believes those. We're doomed."

"I was being held upside down over a stadium! And then I was trying to write after climbing down thirty floors! It was all I could think of! Perhaps Ether can take me back and I can try again, only this time—"

"I think you've done more than enough already."

Ian shrank back from Hutch's expression. It was cold and hard and closed.

\* \* \*

IAN WAS TAKEN by stretcher to a green tent with a bright-red cross on a white square. He didn't see where Ether had gone.

Inside, a group of military doctors were gathered around a homemade still, sipping martinis. One of them turned around as he was brought in and put his drink down in disgust. "War is hell," he grumbled. "I swear each one they bring in here is younger than the last."

It took the surgeon nearly two painful hours to pull all the pieces of the ACM out of Ian's back and another ten minutes or so to get his ankle wrapped. They handed him a crutch and sent him on his way to make room for new patients coming in.

Hobbling along the bumpy turf in the pale lights illuminating the medical compound, Ian found a stack of supply boxes along the pathway and sat down on the nearest one. In the relative quiet away from the front and in the stillness of the night, he could hear the conversations across the encampment, and he could tell the minute the news about the Creature and the Other Sider Who Made Him arrived. Hushed voices became louder, disbelieving and then disgusted.

He leaned back against the boxes and grimaced as something poked his leg through the cloth of a pocket. He pulled it out. It was the notebook he'd brought with him to write down things that might inspire his next game. The metal spiral binding at the top had worked a few loops loose, and they had been bent out of shape in the crash.

He flashed back to Ether cradling his crumpled wing, biting his lip to stay silent against the pain, and then Hutch's quiet fury. Ian's whole leg throbbed angrily now, in time with the distant, terrible heartbeat of Cotwo.

When the sobs came at last, he threw the notebook as hard as he could and heard it hit a puddle somewhere in the distance.

* * *

IAN SLEPT BADLY, propped against the hard stack of crates, his injured leg stretched out before him.

Fighting seemed to resume at first light; the sun had

barely begun to peep over the horizon before the noise from the battlefield started up.

He rubbed his face. His eyes were gritty and heavy, and everything ached. Ian supposed he should go find some food and something to drink, but he couldn't bring himself to move.

The first wave of casualties came in about an hour later. Orderlies dashed from tent to tent, bringing supplies, moving patients, shouting at one another, and cursing as the pace increased. Soon the number of patients coming in was more than the medical staff could cope with, and they had to be lined up on the grounds, groaning and writhing in place.

At some point mid-morning, a tree near the compound exploded, and then another, and another. Local residents began streaming through the makeshift hospital area, panicking in their haste to get away from the violence. Very quickly it became impossible for anyone to work in the hospital, and patients were in danger of being trampled. The call went up to bug out.

Ian roused himself enough to limp over to a supply vehicle and hop on the back before it drove away. When they finally stopped moving, he hopped off and joined a group of other characters recovering in the open air; there simply weren't enough beds for any but the most critically injured.

No one spoke to him. In fact, as soon as he showed up, the whispering began, and anyone near where he chose to sit edged away. He wasn't sure how it was they could tell he was not from the Connectome—something to do with the ethe-reality that Hutch had mentioned, he guessed—but he didn't much care. Ian wasn't even sure he could muster enough energy to defend himself if someone decided to thump him.

They had bunked down next to a beautiful stream, sparkling and flashing in the morning light. By noon, it began to smell of sulphur and something else that Ian couldn't identify. Within a couple more hours, it had clouded, and rainbows slicked its surface.

By nightfall, a large group of trolls had broken through Simian's line. Ian could see them skulking at the edges of the camp, observing and muttering among themselves. He watched as, one by one, they shapeshifted to look like his fellow patients and then casually walked into the compound to sit with them. Ian closed his eyes and tried to sleep. He could hear them whispering as he faded in and out.

"Isn't all this darkness lovely? We need it, you know, as a contrast to the light. The nocturnal critters use it too to survive."

"You know, I haven't seen much evidence of any conflict. I think the council is exaggerating as an excuse to raise taxes. Don't you?"

"I've done my research. This has all happened before. We'll be fine."

"Look at this thing. The Creature made this for us. It's so lovely. It will make your life easier. Don't you want it so much? We need these nice things."

Ian lay down on his side and curled into a ball.

* * *

THE NEXT DAY dawned unbearably hot. The camp was ridiculously overcrowded, as another group of frightened locals had arrived and were demanding food and water. Arguments broke out as frustrations boiled over. Pushing and shouting changed into an all-out brawl that took six military personnel to break up. Ian blinked slowly as he watched, unbelieving. Everything seemed to be falling to pieces so quickly.

Ian's own thirst finally pushed him to go find something to drink. He wobbled over to the line that had formed in front of an increasingly panicked-looking orderly who was carefully doling out water from a dwindling supply. By the time Ian got his drink, he was sweating heavily and feeling light-headed. He walked unsteadily over to the shade of a tree by the stream and put his head between his knees until the awful spinning sensation stopped. He forced himself to sip the cool beverage slowly.

A group of children came into the camp, their faces pale and streaked with tears. Some of them held hands and glanced about uncertainly. One was shivering, in spite of the heat, clearly in shock. Their leader, a tiny girl who looked to be no more than four, shouted with relief when she saw the stream. They all tottered to the bank and started climbing down it, dipping in hands to drink.

Something snapped inside Ian.

"Wait!" he shouted. They jumped guiltily as children do when caught doing something that might be naughty. A couple of them raised their chins defiantly.

"Wait," he said again, beckoning. "That's dirty. Come drink this. I'm going to get you some more." They climbed back up warily, but the offer of a drink proved stronger than their reluctance. He got them settled in the shade with his cup and, taking the shivering boy in his arms, struck out in search of help.

* * *

IT WAS evening by the time Ian managed to get back up to the command post. The pending sunset brought little relief, as there was no breeze and the air was thick with humidity. He found Simian's tent and was dismayed to see that it had a large hole burned through the roof.

All the members of the committee were seated around a folding table with a broken leg; it was being propped up with a spent ooblek cartridge. They looked haggard and battered, and it was plain that none of them had slept much. Ian supposed he didn't look too much better. There were a few other officers from the military whom Ian didn't recognize. And Ether was there, his wing in an incredibly creative set of splints and braces. Ian let out a breath he hadn't realized he'd been holding.

" . . . our last night of darkness. From here on in, there will be more moonlight, so we can probably expect no breaks in—" Simian ground to a halt as Ian straightened from ducking through the tent flap.

There was a long, awkward silence. Eventually, Hutch crossed his nut-brown arms and sniffed. "If this is the bit where you, the outsider, come and try to show us natives how you're going to singlehandedly win the war, we ain't interested."

Ian found a chair and, when no one objected very much, sat down with them. "I do have some ideas," he admitted. "But mostly I'm here to ask your forgiveness for my role in this fiasco."

More silence. Hutch pointedly shifted in his seat to present a shoulder to Ian.

"That's it? You're not even going to yell at me? Just silence?"

"What would you have us say, old man?" Simian said. "We're looking at the destruction and elimination of everything we hold dear."

Ian sighed and nodded. He'd been expecting at least this much. "Look, I'm not perfect. I will cop to being responsible for Cotwo. I will even go so far as to say that I made him and knew even as I was doing so that it was not a great contribution. That it was a decent, *kind* of escapist game but that it wasn't going to do anyone any real good in the long run. It was depressing and defeatist, and probably most of the merch from that game is in landfills by now." Ian swallowed. "I was trying to make a name for myself and make a living, and I didn't stop to think much about how I could have done it differently. Even after I was fired, I concentrated on putting one foot in front of the other, trying not to think too far beyond the next day."

He paused and leaned forward, resting his elbows on his knees. After a few more minutes of silence, he said, "You know, I once read this book about the people who survived the Second World War and the Holocaust. There was one quote that stuck with me. This guy, he said, 'Never underestimate how quickly your world can turn completely upside down.' It's like, one day it all seems hunky-dory, and then next, bam, it's in a shambles. Except, when I thought about it, when you read the history, it's not really sudden . . . not if we're honest. The signs were all there, we just ignored them." Ian scratched his chin and was somewhat surprised to find a scruffy beard. "How much has the Badlands expanded to?"

"Seventy percent," Pixie said quietly.

The number rocked Ian, even so. He sucked in a breath sharply. "Okay. Okay. So, I'm responsible. Yes. But the Creature isn't the only thing out there. I'm not the only one who's done stuff. And the council knew how bad it was getting. Some other people did too. Lots of them. Nobody listened."

Ether looked down.

"So, we didn't fight soon enough or hard enough, and now it's come to this," Ian indicated the tattered tent. "None of us has been perfect, me most of all. But if we don't do something, we'll lose the entire Connectome. I've seen it. It's beautiful. It's *amazing*. It's worth saving."

"There's no magic bullet, is there?" said Heis hesitantly. "No place we can evacuate to? No one to come rescue us?"

"No. Not even Ian's aliens." Hutch snorted. "This is it. We don't have a Plan B."

"We have been trying, Ian," the general said. "But this mess is so big, and the Creature is so tall." He gestured helplessly. "We're down to arguing about which of the last few tricks up our sleeve to try. And I'm sure you've seen how people are beginning to act, starting to fight over what they see as scraps. I'm certain the Creature's minions are actively encouraging that. It's only going to get worse."

"Why pick which one thing to use next? We should throw *everything* at it," Ian said. "All of us together. All at once. And we're going to have to go to the source."

"What? You mean down that hole?" Pixie looked astonished.

"Yes," Ian said. "Down the hole."

Suddenly, Will slammed his fist down on the table, making everyone jump. "Let's do this thing!"

The committee members exchanged glances.

"What?" Will rubbed his fist. "Why does everyone always look at me funny when I do something like that?"

* * *

SIMIAN LEFT grim but clear instructions to his commanders: hold the line—*whatever* the cost. They grabbed weapons and supplies, piled into the Jabberwalk, and galumphed out into the night. Pixie pressed the throttle as far forward as it would go, and Ian had to hold on for dear life.

They skidded to a stop outside Bureaucracy Prime, throwing up clods of dirt and loose stones. Pixie checked her VRML map. A spot at the back of the building was marked "Top Secret Safety Bunker."

"That's our target." Simian adjusted his beret. "Will, Heis, Flanders, you have your orders. Go. Ether, Pixie, Hutch, and Ian, you're with me."

They split up, Simian's party making the long journey

around to the rear of the complex. They found the thin outline of a door and an electronic lock consisting of arrow keys and two buttons labelled A and B.

"Blast!" said Pixie. "I was counting on a lock I could pick."

"I could try freezing the mechanism?" Ether said.

But Ian was smiling. "I got this," he said and cracked his knuckles. He walked up to the console. "Up, up, down, down, left, right, left, right, B, A." The door swung open on exceptionally noisy hinges.

"How did you—?" Ether began.

Ian held up a hand. "Old school. Thank my misspent youth. Come on."

They pounded down endless stairs that eventually opened up into a long, cold tunnel. At the end, they found the entrance to the bunker was sealed with a thick layer of red tape.

"Gaaaaaah," Ether rumbled. "We do *not* have time for this!"

"Oooh, oooh!" Hutch hopped up and down. "General, may I? I got something from R's lab that I've been dying to try."

"Got? Or swiped?"

"That depends on who's asking."

The general gave him a disapproving look. "Desperate times, I suppose. Tally ho then."

Hutch laughed maniacally and pulled a short length of hose from his backpack. Ian realized it wasn't a pack at all, but a tank.

"Whoa," Ian said. "Hit the deck!"

Everyone but the rabbit fell back. Hutch pulled on a pair of welding goggles. The end of his hose bloomed red, and a blast of heat washed over them. A second later, the remains of the charred red tape fluttered to the floor.

They cautiously drew level with Hutch, who was trembling with excitement and shedding fine particles of soot in a ring around his feet.

"Well done, my leporine friend," Simian said. "Pity about your whiskers." He pulled out a handkerchief, wrapped it a few times around his hand, and carefully pulled the door open.

Inside, the councillors barely spared them a glance as they filed in.

"Agenda item 454," the old man with the lapels droned. "Economic outlook report."

Adonis yawned hugely. "Please spare us your latest numbers and just spit out the latest job creation scheme, why don't you?"

The old man looked affronted. "The numbers are important! We must keep employment up! Why, in the southern half of my constituency—"

"Point of Order!" Ether interjected.

"What? Weren't you in here before? Did you see the clerk about getting on the agenda?"

"The southern half of your constituency no longer exists."

"Oh." The old man was nonplussed. But then he smiled. "That effectively doubles my campaign budget!"

"Council," Ian said before they could get bogged down again, "you *must* release more resources to push back the Badlands. We're losing the fight."

Hagar looked at him over a pair of reading glasses. "Ah, the Other Sider. I'm sure you mean well, but we're still gathering data. There are a few experts out of seven hundred who don't agree that there's a problem. We don't want to do anything too drastic that might upset the balance here. Much as I hate to agree with my colleague—"

"Point of Order," Ether said.

"What again? This is highly irregular. I don't think Robert's Rules—"

"Stuff Robert," the dragon growled. "Do you have a viewer in here?"

"Why yes, there's a camera system to, er, monitor the situation right outside the building."

"Turn it on," Simian said.

"Fine, eh?" Joe wandered over to a viewer on the wall and turned it on. The screen filled with the image of an angry crowd, all of them sporting protest signs and shouting slogans about voting out every single council member.

Adonis blanched.

Ian leaned over to Ether. "How the heck did they manage to rally that many people that fast?" he hissed.

"Heis' specialty." Ether winked. "Action at a distance."

"That's spooky."

"But useful."

Back around the council table, there was a growing sense of panic. "Like, omigod," Babs said, consulting her stone tablet. "I'm getting messages from, like, everywhere. The voting public seems . . . super cheesed."

"Good gravy," Mr. Lapels said, reading his own. "Some of them are suggesting they won't even wait until an election. They . . . they want to throw peaches at us?"

"Oooh! Maybe I should stick around." Ether rubbed his claws together.

"I think he means impeachment," Ian said. "Sorry. Although the other could be just as fun."

"Motion to convene a special emergency meeting of the Finance and Resource Subcommittee?" said Hagar.

"Seconded, eh?'

"All in favour?" Adonis asked. All council hands shot up. "Let's discuss this. Behind closed doors," he added, glaring at the intruders.

Ether offered Ian a fist bump. "Phase one is a success!"

* * *

ON THE WAY back to the command post, backpacks laden with council orders and procurement forms, they stopped at the edge of the forest.

"Why here, General?" Ian asked.

"You said you wanted to get in touch with that bush, as I recall?"

"Yes, but it was way over near the original Badlands border, wasn't it?"

Simian led them into the trees. "Indeed. But I rather think we'll have a job trying to get back there now. There's a fungus box ahead, though."

"A . . . fungus box?"

Simian pointed. There, between two old trees, was a classic red phone booth. Only when Ian looked closer, it wasn't totally red. It had white spots that glowed softly all over it just like the top of the iconic toadstools he'd seen in books as a kid.

At this stage, nothing was surprising Ian much. He shrugged. "I'm lichen it. How do I use it?"

"Mycelium network. Pixie should be able to give you the dial-up coordinates."

"Hmm," Ian said. "Will he pick up though? He was really grumpy and didn't seem like a very fun—"

Ether stopped him with a hand on the shoulder. "Ian. There are limits, even here."

"Fair enough," Ian said and went to the box. It opened softly and he stepped in. The receiver was soft and spongy. "Ick. Gimme the number."

The bush picked up only after Ian let it ring for a full minute.

"Fer cryin' out loud, *what?*"

"Hello, old friend."

"Oh, it's you. Whaddya want, Sparky?"

"Funny you should call me that," Ian said. "You remember how I said I would come in hot if I had to see you again?"

"What? I didn't steer you wrong last time. You got no beef with me."

"For now," Ian conceded. "But to keep it that way, you're going to do me a favour." Ian could tell the bush was flouncing indignantly.

"You're annoying," the bush whined. "But I suppose you won't let up until you get what you want. Fine. What?"

"I need you to get rid of this black fog everywhere."

"Jeez Louise, you don't want much. How am I supposed to do that?"

"Have you and your friends," Ian said down the line, "ever heard of a leaf vacuum?"

* * *

BACK AT THE COMMAND POST, Simian's troops were busy fighting a battle on two fronts. Rioting had broken out amongst the residents, and it was all the soldiers could do to keep the various factions that had sprung up from killing each other.

Using binoculars, Ian scanned one of the crowds. "There," he pointed, handing the device back to Flanders. "Watch the one in the green shirt."

"He's right, General," Flanders concurred. "Theah ah definitely trolls working everybody up into a latha."

"I think that's what Phil must have meant," Heis said. "Maybe."

Pixie frowned. "We need to ice-block those trolls. Ether?"

"I'm sure willing to try," Ether said, gently flexing his wing and wincing. "With a bit more wing reinforcement. But even without an injury, I couldn't do it all alone."

Private Hemloch suddenly stepped out of the shadows, making Will yelp.

Simian swore. "Good God, man. Why aren't you dead yet?"

"Sorry, sir, I keep trying, sir. I came to report that we have just had a large contingent of dragons volunteer to help out. Shall I send their leader in?"

"I suppose so. Now, Ether, you were saying?"

"Only that there are bound to be a lot of these trolls. I'm going to need some sort of detection device from R to spot them more easily and agghduuhhhh . . ."

Ian turned around. The leader of the volunteer dragons had arrived. She was long, sleek, beautiful, and a gorgeous tone of red.

"Hello, General," she said in a voice that even Ian found attractive. "We'd like to help. We didn't volunteer before because we didn't think we could be much use, but it seems to be getting fairly desperate out here."

"Ginger, I presume," said Ian, grinning.

"Mmumbledurrrmumblegleep," said Ether, looking completely gobsmacked.

"We could use all the help we can get." Simian shook her claw. "What made you think you couldn't be of much help before?"

"Well, we're not the standard kind of dragon with flames and so on," she said, looking slightly embarrassed. "I blow freezing confetti, you see. Probably great for a wedding on a hot day, but . . ."

"Really?" Ian raised a delighted eyebrow at Ether.

"Jolly good," said Simian. "As it happens, we've got just the assignment for you. Ginger, meet Ether."

"Arglebarglebinkle," Ether said, unable to take his eyes off Ginger.

"Um, is he okay?" Ginger looked at Ian.

"Took a blow to the head in the fighting. He'll be fine as soon as the blood starts flowing in the right direction again." He walked over to Ether to put an arm around his shoulder, simultaneously treading heavily on a dragon foot.

"Mumbleowowow. Er . . . hi, Ginger," Ether said rather breathlessly. "It's ridiculously good to meet you. Walk with me?"

\* \* \*

"NEXT PHASE?" said the general.

"Right," Ian replied. "Who haven't we called to help yet?"

Will ticked them off on his fingers. "The misfit toys. Also the Lost Boys, the Laputans, and the mooses. Moosi? Whatever."

"That's the islands taken care of," Simian said. "Go send messages, Will. Who else?"

"What about the plucky British schoolchildren?" Pixie said. "They're always good in a crisis."

"Crikey, has it come to that?" Simian sighed. "I suppose it has. Make it so, Pixie. Hutch?"

"My cousin Sixer has some pull in the rabbit community. I can see who he can rally."

"Excellent. Have them report to Flanders at the bridge into Technocity. If that falls, we've really had it."

"What about the dogs, sir?" Hemloch suggested.

"Not a bad idea. See to it."

Hemloch spun on his heel, stuck two fingers into his mouth, and let out the longest, loudest, most piercing whistle Ian had ever heard in his life. Then Hemloch shouted, "TIM-MY'S DOWN A WELL!"

When everyone's ears had stopped ringing, Simian spoke. "Hemlock?"

"Sir?"

"Next time, perhaps you could do that, you know, away from here?"

"Sorry, sir. And it's Hemloch, sir."

In the distance, Ian could hear dogs baying. "You'll be calling for cats next, at this rate."

"Excellent idea. Heis, make preparations for that. And now," Simian said, casting a deeply worried glance at Pixie. "I think it's time for you to make your descent, ladies and gentlemen. Let's find out what we're dealing with."

\* \* \*

AN HOUR LATER, Will, Ian, Heis, and Pixie, dressed all in black and with faces painted dark, were scrambling as quickly as they could along a creek bank. Pixie, using her map, had worked out that the creek cut right through the Badlanders' current position, and further, that it had swollen enough with the recent storms that the rushing water made an excellent cover noise. The only problem was that it was thick with brush and slick. It was also very dark, and the night-vision spectacles that R had given them only did so much. Ian had come close to spraining his other ankle twice now and had almost fallen in once.

Pixie, in the lead, held up a fist. They stumbled to a stop and crouched low while she checked their position. Then she gestured for everyone to climb the bank and peek over the top.

The pounding beat of the Creature was thunderous here. In the sickly green field of view provided by the spectacles, Ian could see it crouching and pulsing, waiting impatiently for first light to renew its attack. Apparently, it had no need for sleep.

They ducked back down the bank. "I-I-I'm not so sure about this," Will whispered.

"We have no choice," Ian said. "Although I was kind of hoping it would be snoozing instead of waiting."

"The creatures around it are sleeping," Pixie said. "It looks like all the nocturnals are at their perimeter patrolling."

"Or worse, infiltrating *our* position. Maybe," said Heis.

"Focus on the problem in front of us," Ian said. "Can we get directly behind Cotwo, run for it, and drop down the hole?"

"Going to have to be something like that," said Pixie, pulling off her backpack. "But I don't want to just jump in. We have no idea how deep that thing is or where it goes."

"I need chocolate," Will fretted.

"Promise you some when this is all over." Pixie tied one end of a long rope around Will's waist. "Right now, you're the fastest and lightest of all of us, so you're jumping in first. The other end of this is going around this tree. Tug it twice when you think it's safe for us to climb down after you. Heis, circle off to the side and prepare to create some noise for a distraction if need be."

"Got it. I think."

"*Go!*"

* * *

WILL PELTED ACROSS THE TURF, leaping over the sleeping forms at the base of the Creature's hole, closed his eyes, and flung himself down it belly-flop style.

"Dun Dun Dun da dada Dun dun dun da dada dun dun dun da dada . . ."

He plunged into the abyss.

"Dun Dun DUN da dada Dun dun DUN da dada dun dun dun da dada . . ."

The rope played out farther, faster.

"DUN DUN DUN da dada Dun dun DUN da dada dun dun dun da dada . . ."

The rope tightened at the base of the tree, caught him, stretched, and creaked. He stopped in a spread-eagle position just centimetres from the ground. He reached down from his splayed-out position, touched the earth before springing up again, and settled with a soft thud against the wall. Will tugged the rope twice.

"DUN DUN DUN DA DADA DUN DUN DUN DA DADA DUN DUN DUN DA DADA . . ."

"Will!" Pixie rasped from above.

"Yes?"

"Shut *up*."

"Sorry."

"This mission is damn near impossible as it is. We don't need you giving our position away!"

"I said I'm sorry!"

Ian and Pixie climbed down the rope, their combined weight stretching the cord down again. They untied him and waited for Heis to slither down after them.

They waited for several minutes for some sort of alarm or sign that they had been detected. Ian decided to risk a flashlight. He cursed when his spectacles blazed bright green and propped them up on top of his head.

Directly before them was an enormous machine, the front of which was a giant set of slashing, grinding blades for chewing and eating the earth and bedrock. Behind the blades, the machine's prodigious maw was obviously meant to take in the crushed material and crunch it down further. Cautiously, they followed the works backward. Several exhausts coated in filth—the source of the black fog—pointed directly up the hole. A thin stream of it was still curling up into the night. The entire thing reeked of machine oil, overheated metal and rock, and engine fumes.

Trailing the exhausts was a large processing box that took material in the front and had observation windows coated in muck. Pixie rubbed one clean. A large set of teeth attached to a squirming larval brute slammed into the window. Pixie yowled and jumped away. Ian heard its teeth grinding against the glass and shivered.

Another processing box seemed to produce the trinkets and nice things that the trolls had been offering. The final box made Ian frown in puzzlement. It took the tailings and pressed them into a bright-red liquid that was then bottled. "Well, it's efficient, I'll say that," he said.

"Shh," Pixie said. "Listen."

From farther down the tunnel, they could hear music. It was loud, discordant, and heavy on the guitar.

"Death metal," Ian said and shrugged when Pixie looked askance. "Another phase of my youth."

They followed the sound down the tunnel and around a bend, where they found a long, black multi-car vehicle that looked a lot like a train polished to a high gloss. It had stopped for the night, and there was definitely a party going on.

They slunk along the side of the train until they discovered a set of windows that didn't have the shades pulled. They peeped in. Dozens of vampires and other members of the Badlander haut monde, dressed in opulent clothing, were dancing, shouting, and drinking. Bottles of the red stuff were everywhere.

One of them happened to glance in the direction of the window and glared. He staggered toward them to look closer. They ducked away and ran for the bottom of the hole again.

"Okay," Ian breathed, "we know what's powering the fog, the proto creatures, and maybe Cotwo as well. How do we stop it?"

"We need Ether down here," Pixie said. "I have an idea. And then we need your everything-at-once phase, Ian. Help me put up a camera here so we can keep an eye on them."

\* \* \*

PIXIE SENT Heis to fetch Ether. The tiny pink dragon grew to human size after he'd tumbled down the hole.

"Guys, guys, GUYS!" Ether panted. "I got her number!" He wriggled with glee.

"That's awesome, Ether." Pixie smiled. "We might want to try to save the Connectome before date night though."

"Oh, right." The dragon settled down. "What do you need?"

"I want you to quietly lay down a long trail of glitter on either side of this train thing back here. Not too thick. And then help us get back to the command post."

"Huh? Okay. Whatever you say."

\* \* \*

NOT LONG BEFORE DAWN, they arrived back at command without too much issue. Ian palmed his eyes, trying to make the heaviness go away. Pixie debriefed Simian on what they'd found and done.

"That's the best news I've had all week," Simian beamed. "Capital. I know exactly what I'm going to do with that intel too." He strode out of the tent. "COs! On me! It's time we took the initiative and stopped fighting on a rearguard basis."

"WAIT!"

Someone stepped out of the crowd of homeless local residents that had been milling around.

"Is this a good idea? What if we're wrong? This is a lot of effort and expense. Maybe we should just let them come.

Where will we get nice things like this?" He held up something that Ian recognized as one of the baubles from the vampires and looked at it sadly.

Will led him away gently. "There, there. I know you heard stuff from the trolls, but don't worry, we'll still have nice things. Some of them may even be shiny…"

"Right, where was I?" Simian yanked down his tunic. "First, we shore up defences. Signal Flanders."

"Sir!"

* * *

IAN CHECKED the monitor set up for Flanders' team. Way off in the distance, at the largest bridge into Technocity on the Badlanders' side, Flanders stood in front of a massive crowd of rabbits. He looked a little uncertain about some of them, given that a lot of them had glowing red eyes and sharp teeth that made them look a lot like the vampires, but they had shown up and were obeying orders, and that's all he needed.

An out-of-breath infantryman ran up and stopped in front of him. "We've received the signal to blow the bridge, Colonel."

"Right!" Flanders clucked. He addressed the crowd. "Hop to it!"

The rabbits marched as one onto the end of the bridge. Then one at the front shouted, "Danger!" and began thumping his hind leg.

Others quickly followed. Soon all of them were thumping, and then after a few minutes, the chaotic pounding resolved into a single, synchronized beat. The bridge began to vibrate. The lead rabbit crouched a bit, squinted to watch the bridge, and adjusted his thump rate to match it. A wave of change washed through the rabbits as they matched him. The bridge started to shake in earnest and then warp and buckle. The pounding slowed, harmonizing with the large sine waves that were now reverberating through the structure. The leader's paw went up, and the rabbits thumped harder.

The bridge disintegrated. A cheer resounded, and the rabbits started high-fiving each other's ears.

Flanders smiled for the first time in a while.

\* \* \*

BACK AT COMMAND, Simian raised his arm and then dropped it. Working in formation, a dozen soldiers bearing tuna cans and can openers marched up to a dozen more soldiers holding megaphones. As one, they set the cans to open, little motors whirring into the amplifiers.

In the distance, there was an ominous rumbling from the direction of the Flux.

Simian turned in another direction. "Release the hounds!" he bellowed.

All the dogs that Hemloch had summoned earlier suddenly barreled out from behind command. There were three-headed dogs with slavering jaws, lots of fluffy mixed-breed pooches, dozens of Collies, several big red dogs, and hundreds of Dalmatians.

"Fetch!" Simian cried.

The dogs charged the battlefield in the dim light, bringing down orcs, trolls, and demons. Several of the scare bears were shaken into pieces.

"Bad dog! Not a squeaky! No! No fetch! Argh!"

The cats arrived.

Anyone the dogs hadn't caught yet, the cats tripped. Many of them rolled on the ground, looking playful, and then ripped off the appendages of any of the Badlanders unwise enough to try to stroke them.

"Look!" Ian shouted, pointing.

The trees had come. There were slow, ponderous oaks, sad little willows, giant pounding sequoias and baobabs, lithe and almost musical bamboo, and scuttling underbrush. They all had leaf vacuums, and they all turned them on at once and started sucking up the fog.

Ian covered his ears. The roaring, whooshing noise was even louder than the cats and dogs.

\* \* \*

ON THE VIEW screen that broadcast from where they planted the camera underneath the battlefield, they could see something was up. The party train had stopped rocking, as someone must have gotten suspicious and thought to turn down the music for a minute. Ian could see a pair that he thought were Lestatler and Wooldorf. They had stopped dancing, bewildered, and then glowered as they heard the chaos above.

"How DARE they!" Wooldorf snarled. He ran up to the front of the train car, pulled open a panel, and slammed some switches. The machine in the hole clanked to life and started chewing the earth and belching blackness.

"Let's crush them!" Lestatler kicked a car door open. The vampires all along the train poured out into the tunnel and stopped undead in their tracks.

"Ooooh!"

"Aaah!"

"So pretty!"

"Glitter!"

"Must . . . count . . . them . . ."

"One, two, three, four . . ."

" . . . twenty-six, twenty-seven . . ."

\* \* \*

THE CREATURE HAD ROUSED. And it was angry.

It was also confused.

It roared and blew up several trees. Cats went flying everywhere as it kicked. It turned this way and that, not sure what to target.

"Dragons!" Simian called. "Take flight!"

"Once more into its breeches!" Ether responded. "Chaaaarge!"

The sky filled with dragons. Ether's group attacked the ground troops, while a smaller contingent of bright-orange dragons headed straight for Cotwo. They swarmed him, blowing—Ian leaned forward to see—soap bubbles. Soon the Creature was a seething, sliding, frothing mess.

From the east, another platoon of rabbits charged in. Unable to contain himself, Hutch quivered to attention and then raced out to join the assault. They launched themselves at the Creature's ankles, gnawing as hard as they could. Cotwo, now blinded by the soap in its eyes, howled in pain.

Above ground, Simian blew a whistle. "Who's a good dog, then?"

Hundreds of dogs stopped what they were doing, cocked their heads, and whined. The cats all stopped too but proceeded to lick their paws disdainfully, rather than paying attention to any commands.

"Dig!" Simian said.

Barking excitedly, the dogs immediately set to burrowing into the ground. The cats shrieked in disgust and scattered as dirt went flying everywhere.

It took a while, but the dogs eventually exposed the tunnel, and the dirt collapsed all around the train.

". . . forty-two thousand twenty-one . . . forty-two thousand twenty-two . . ."

The sun slipped over the horizon as dawn broke.

" . . . forty-two thousand twenty-three . . . forty-two
AAAAAAH THE SUN!!"

Vampires began disintegrating into dust. Some of them
tried to dive back into the train, but the dogs gleefully gave
chase and dragged them back out by their pant legs. Ether
and Ginger broke off their ground attack and flew down into
the hole behind Cotwo. Working together, they blew into the
works of the machine wherever they could, filling it with
frozen glitter and confetti until it sparkled and gleamed. The
gears ground to a loud, screeching halt.

Then, for no apparent reason, the cats went berserk,
darting and running every which way, adding to the
mayhem. Hundreds of them ran up the Creature, biting and
slashing and shredding.

Deprived of its power source and overwhelmed, the black
fog dissipating as the trees advanced, Cotwo toppled backward onto the train and lay still. The Badlanders who were
still standing began to run.

* * *

THE COMMAND POST exploded into cheers, hugs, and laughter. Simian and Pixie hugged for far longer than was deco-
rous, but nobody cared. Ether, Ginger, and Hutch staggered
back to the tent, and Flanders sent word that he was coming
back in and expected a party.

Simian sobered quickly. "All well and good to think that,
but any celebrations will have to be very short-lived. We've a
devil of a job ahead of us in terms of clean-up and
restoration."

They looked around. The battlefield was a shambles, and
the landscape beyond was a blackened ruin. The trees had
sustained heavy damage and were struggling to keep up with

the fog, even with the machine no longer producing it. Many of the animals were broken and bleeding. The medical teams were already exhausted and struggling from the previous days of fighting.

"The Flux," Ian said suddenly. "Is it still up? That's going to be the only way to repopulate the Connectome, isn't it?"

"It is, I believe," Heis replied. "I was there as well as here, I think."

They all let out a relieved sigh.

Simian reassigned a platoon of soldiers to round up civilian volunteers and put them to work. "It's going to take all of us," he said, seeing them off.

Will stood with his legs spread and arms akimbo, looking out over the wreckage. "We can do this," he said, nodding confidently.

And this time, no one turned to stare.

\* \* \*

THEY WERE BREAKING for lunch when Private Hemloch reported back in. Pixie giggled at Simian's expression.

"You survived the entire bloody war," Simian said dryly.

"Oh, yes, sir. I think I worked out how."

"Do tell."

"Well, actually, statistically speaking, *gold* shirts are much more likely to die on a mission. So the odds were ever in my favour."

"Ack," said Ian.

"Ack indeed," said Simian.

\* \* \*

THE NEXT MORNING, Pixie looked at him with watery eyes, and even Hutch sniffled a little more than necessary for someone with a cold.

"You're sure you have to go, my boy?" Simian asked him. "It's been jolly good having you around. You came through for us when it counted too."

"W-w-we'll miss you," Will agreed.

"Absolutely," Heis said.

Ian smiled at them all. "I really should go back. I belong on the Other Side, and there are things I have to do."

"Well, let me assure you," Flanders said, "that my doah is always open should you decide to come back for a visit."

Everyone nodded. "Mine too," they said.

Ian felt his own eyes tearing up but pushed on. "The same goes for my door." He waved sadly and walked over to where Ether awaited him.

The dragon immediately puddled up.

"Jeez, Ether, don't *you* start," Ian grumbled, wiping his eyes surreptitiously.

"It won't be the same without you, Ian," Ether snuffled. "You won't stay?"

"I can't, Ether." Ian reached out a hand to pat the dragon's shoulder. "I've got a mess to clean up too. My visit here has taught me many things, and I need to take them back with me. "

Ether grinned. "Like how to get over your fear of heights?"

"I didn't have a fear of heights until I met you, idiot."

"Then what?"

Ian pondered. "Like why I liked Pixie so much, for one thing."

Ether wiggled his eyebrows. "Why's that?"

Now Ian grinned. "She reminds me of someone I know, and it's time I did something about it."

"Hubba hubba!" Ether playfully cuffed Ian, bruising him in several places.

"Which reminds me," Ian said. "Are you going to be doing something about a certain lady dragon I've heard so much about? Now that you've got her number?"

"Awwww, Ian!" Ether blushed and scuffed his toes against the ground.

"Don't get all bashful on me, big guy." Ian pulled Ether's chin up to look him directly in the eye. "There's no reason in the world why she wouldn't go out with you. You're smart, funny, strong, resourceful, and one heck of a dragon."

"Really?"

"Really," Ian said firmly. "And the next time you visit, I want to hear all about your first date. So make that call."

"The next time I visit?"

"I've already made plans to lay in a supply of peaches. Bring a box of those research notes and we'll make a weekend of it."

"Woohoo!" Ether shouted. "I'll be there with bells on."

Ian reached in for a hug. "Goodbye, Ether."

"Goodbye, Ian." Ether hugged him back and then waved a hand to open a rift.

Ian was about to step through when a bush fluttered over to quiver in front of him. Ian looked closely. It looked like *the* bush, but it was hard to tell.

"So, uh," it said, "we square? No more threats? No fiery retribution?"

Ian nodded. "Square."

"Good." It fumbled around a bit and then handed Ian his muddy, still slightly damp notebook of ideas. "You must have dropped this someplace. Now you owe *me* one, wise guy."

Ian laughed, saluted his thanks, and stepped through the rift.

\* \* \*

WHEN HE CAME TO, Ian found himself face-down on the field. He spat out bits of dirt and leaves.

He sat up, trying to remember where he was. He looked down at his clothes—ordinary jeans and his rugby shirt. He checked his arms. They were gash- and bruise-free.

He squished through the soft earth and found his truck. It looked as old and battered as usual.

"Damn," he said, the crushing weight of disappointment falling on him. "It was all . . . just a *dream*. Damn . . ."

He got into the truck and drove into town. His house looked as it always had.

Ian checked the kitchen, but it was clean, and the towels were still in the corner from when he had cleaned up the water leak. He walked into his living room, and the computer still sat there with the word-processing software open, the little cursor still blinking away.

He slumped into the chair.

"Damn," he said again softly.

The phone rang.

"Hello?"

"Ian! Ian, is that you? Where have you been? Mrs. Wilson saw you pull in with the truck!"

"Janice?"

"Yes. Janice. You know . . . your employer? And, I thought, your friend? Where have you been? Are you okay?"

"I'm fine," Ian said, looking around the room more carefully now. "How long have I—" He caught sight of something on the shelves. "Hang on." He put the phone down and walked over to it.

Beside his old game, there was a new, large, hardcover book that he didn't recognize. He picked it up and flipped through it. The pages were all blank. He checked the front cover.

" ," it said, "by Ian McDonald."

Ian smiled.

He picked up the phone again. "Janice? Hello? You still there?"

"Yes, Ian. What's *wrong*? Are you okay? I've been worried sick about you!"

"Janice, I . . ." Ian hesitated. "I've had a life-changing experience."

"You're not on drugs or something, are you?"

Ian laughed. "No, no. Listen, I'd like to tell you all about it. I owe you an explanation for one thing, and besides, there are a few things I want to ask you about. What are you doing for dinner tonight?"

There was a long pause at the other end. "Nothing, I guess," she said finally. "Are you . . . are you asking me out?"

"Yes," Ian said, grinning like a fool. "Come on over around six. I'll cook."

"Okay," Janice said uncertainly.

When he hung up the phone, Ian checked the clock. It was half past one.

He cracked his knuckles, rubbed his hand over the empty book, and typed swiftly on the keyboard.

"TO DO LIST," the screen said. And he wrote down all the things he was going to tackle . . . properly, one at a time. The house, the yard, the job, his social life, his finances, and some ideas for volunteer work with the local greening initiative. All of it went on the list. Then he closed that file and started a new one.

"CHAPTER ONE," he began.

He had a lot to write before six.

And it was going to involve dragons. *Hot*-pink dragons.

And pixies. Lots and lots of pixies.

## ABOUT THE AUTHOR

Chandra Clarke wears many hats, sometimes all at once, which makes it hard to get through doorways.

A recovering/relapsing entrepreneur, she will also admit to having been a freelance writer, with publishing credits in places like *Popular Science, Canadian Business*, and yes, even *Voice of the Kent Farmer*. She recently finished a PhD, because she's something of an academic masochist.

She's a mother to four kids and two dogs, and wife to Terry Johnson, the best British import since the Aston Martin. Chandra thinks her family is pretty awesome, but she might be biased.

**If you enjoyed this book, <u>please</u> leave a review where you bought it! Reviews help authors reach other readers, and reviews help readers like you decide what books to buy.**

"Clarke's lush prose envisions a future both alien and utterly believable." — *Kirkus Reviews*

"...an engrossing blend of thriller and hard sci-fi that will delight readers looking for crossovers that pepper social issues and developments into the story line. — D. Donovan, Senior Reviewer, *Midwest Book Review*

"I found the author's vision for the world of tomorrow to be one of my favorite things about Echoes of Another. My other favorite thing about this book is that it's just a really good story told in a way that felt fresh and even cutting edge. "— Scott Cahan, *Readers' Favorite*, 5/5 Stars

"I would highly recommend this book for someone who likes science fiction settings without the heaviness of hard core science fiction. This is a character driven vehicle in a science fiction setting. It doesn't get bogged down in the science. It tells the story of people."— Mimi L., *NetGalley Reviewer* 5/5 Stars

# CHAPTER ONE: RAY

Ray stepped out of the shadows of his apartment block and shivered in the cold.

The sky was beryl blue and clear. The sun was just high enough over the horizon to send brilliant beams of light skittering across the snow, making it sparkle like diamonds. Drifts and rooftop snows had begun to evaporate, wraith mists gently rising into the air.

He tugged his coat collar a little higher. If he had to guess, he figured it was about twenty degrees below freezing. Not so bad, especially for the first week of January, but he knew the buildings lining the downtown could sometimes funnel the cold wind until it howled.

"Summon," he said, enjoying the way his words formed plumes and floated away. The snow squeaked under his feet as he shifted the weight of his short, stocky frame from one to the other nervously. Several anxious moments passed before a single-seater pod emblazoned with the Toronto Transit Commission logo glided around the corner and stopped in front of him. He calmed down a bit, grateful the transponder he'd pickpocketed actually worked. The door opened, and he climbed into the small patch of warmth. There were no controls or amenities, just a thinly cushioned seat showing its age, a restraint that automatically clamped across his lap as soon as he sat down, and a hard, bioplastic dashboard with nothing on it other than an embedded screen. A small heater under the chair blasted hot air at his shoes. There was room enough for him and not much else. His sun visor fogged over from the abrupt change in temperature when the door closed, but he ignored the sudden blurriness, knowing it would clear on its own shortly.

"Destination?" the pod asked, startling him. He'd been expecting to have to tap in a station.

"Uh, Edward. Go by way of Sheppard and Queen's Park Flows please."

The pod nav did a quick calculation. "Estimated arrival time, 7.3 minutes. Entertainment options?"

"Nothing, thanks," he replied. He wouldn't have known what to ask for, anyway. Besides, he wanted to look at the beautiful old university buildings as they zoomed past. Perhaps he'd catch a glimpse of that determined-looking woman with the light-brown hair he had seen there. It would be a good omen, and he needed one. He had a lot riding on getting everything right this morning. This job would change everything.

The pod accelerated, smooth and silent. There was hardly any traffic in his seedy neighbourhood, but as they approached the city core where the buildings were bigger and newer, the trickle of pods became a stream, and then a torrent. He tensed as his pod hurtled towards the major flow that would take him the rest of the way downtown. But the rushing vehicles adjusted, parting to reveal a pod-sized space into which they merged effortlessly. He looked at the dashboard and discovered that the screen showed him his position in real time. He marvelled at the thousands of pods pulsing like white blood cells through the arteries of the city.

Ray tried to relax into his seat, but he was too jittery, and the chair was rather hard and uncomfortable. The pod slowed a little as it neared his destination. Already, he could see people hurrying along the footpaths, their shoulders hunched against the cold. He wondered how many of them were tourists; most city natives knew to use the downtown's underground paths in weather like this.

A familiar face flashed by the window. Startled, he spun around in his seat to look out the back.

"Stop!"

"Emergency stop," the pod replied.

Unfazed by the sudden change of plan, the pod decelerated and pulled carefully onto a footpath, its warning lights flashing brightly. Pedestrians walked around it but otherwise ignored both it and him. Ray wondered how often pods must have to make unplanned stops for it to be so unremarkable. He tumbled out of the pod and jogged back up along Bay Flow, rounding the corner in time to see the man he was looking for duck into an alley off Elm.

"Hey, Mick!" Ray shouted, running faster.

Mick was a tall man now; much different from the gangly, skinny teenager Ray remembered. Mick's long legs and lithe frame meant he took rangy strides and had a fast pace. He was already halfway down the alley when Ray reached the entrance.

"Mick!" Ray shouted again.

Mick stopped and turned, frowning a little. His face broke into a wide, easy grin when he recognised Ray. He waited for him to catch up.

"Hey man," Mick said, pushing a wayward lock of brown hair out of his eyes. He wore a couple of day's growth of beard. "Look at you, all grown up. You're a long way out of J-District, aren't you?"

"I could say the same about you," Ray replied, panting a little after his unexpected sprint. "What happened? You kinda disappeared on me."

"Yeah, I—"

A drone dropped out of nowhere, stopping between them, hovering almost silently. It was big and black and unmarked, and it steamed like a dragon in the frigid air.

It flicked a scanner beam, long and red, a tongue, up the length of Mick, tasting him. Mick's eyes widened in fear.

And then the drone exploded.

* * *

Buy it now at your favourite online retailer:
https://books2read.com/u/m2ZMod